HEATHER BOYD

BESTSELLING AUTHOR

THE DUKE AND I

SAINTS AND SINNERS SERIES

BOOK 1: THE DUKE AND I
BOOK 2: A GENTLEMAN'S VOW

THE DUKE AND I
Copyright © 2017 by Heather Boyd
Edited by Kelli Collins

Dedication

———•———

This story is dedicated to my husband John—
bringer of wisdom, enthusiast of my wild
imaginings, advocate of dreaming big. We do
everything well together, too.

Prologue

———•———

London,
March, 1818

Nicolas Westfall paced the front hall of his middle daughter's Mayfair home, attempting to rein in his temper. Fanny had done it again. Offending an important member of society was no laughing matter. Memories of such impudence lasted years and Nicolas had another daughter to think about too.

Fanny rushed down the stairs of her residence to greet him, smiling widely as she came but he'd bet she was dreading the coming inevitable confrontation over her behavior. She had to know why he'd come. "Father, what an unexpected surprise."

Nicolas regarded Fanny with exasperation.

Of all his daughters, he had a soft spot for her, even if she was the most troublesome of the bunch. She reminded him of his late wife in so many ways. Impulsive, exuberant, and unmindful of many of the rules of society.

Thankfully, Fanny still squirmed under his scrutiny the way she had since a little girl, and that gave him hope that she might listen to his counsel. After all, she was too old to take over his knee to deliver her the scolding she deserved. "Fanny."

"I thought you were still at home in the country," she exclaimed pausing several feet away.

"I had unexpected business in Town." He held open his arms. "Come here, Fanny girl. Give your old father a squeeze before I must scold you."

He *always* tried to prepare his children for when he needed to shout at them. They had no mother. Just Nicolas. He loved them but did not always approve of their choices.

Fanny hurried across the room, hugged him tightly for as long as possible and then slowly drew away from him. She winced. "It is not as terrible a scandal as everyone is saying. Gossip is almost always a vast embellishment of the truth."

He snorted. "You called the Duchess of Lowell an ill-bred old goat…"

"Without a shred of human kindness or decency," Fanny finished for him. "Yes, I admit

I said that."

There were other slanderous remarks she'd made too, but she would only admit to the rest if Nicolas mentioned them first. He knew his daughter well. He pinched the bridge of his nose. Finding a replacement governess for his youngest daughter would have to wait until another day. "Regardless of whether it is true or not you should not have said any of that in a public place," he complained.

"But father it was terrible," she protested. "I couldn't sit idly by while a kind and gentle woman was so ill-used by that woman."

"I'm sure to you it was a grave indignity, but it was none of your concern. Why must you meddle in the affairs of those who can harm your reputation?"

"Well, it had to be someone's concern," Fanny protested. "The way some servants are treated makes my blood boil. I have no regrets. Not one."

She never did. Nicolas hooked her arm through his firmly and led Fanny along to her upstairs parlor. "I'm sure you see it that way, but others most certainly do not. I had dinner at my club last night and the silence on my arrival was extremely awkward, to say the least. Lowell was there and stormed out. You know I like *him*. Now tell me everything about the encounter from the beginning," he demanded.

"I'll do my best to repair the damage you've done if I can."

Fanny explained what she'd found: a governess harried and abused at a coaching inn where she'd stopped for luncheon the previous week. It wasn't an unfamiliar story. Those with power often used it ill.

"Do you know the worst of it? Despite her efforts to please them, despite the beating she received with a parasol no less, Lady Lowell dismissed her there and then. They didn't care if they stranded her in that god-forsaken place. She would have had no position, no reference, and no hope of improving her situation or recovering her possessions from the country."

Fanny was the impulsive one, but she had a great heart for those with less than herself. Which amounted to nearly everyone she met, unfortunately. His daughter had been left a vast fortune by her late husband but thankfully had the brains to manage it competently herself. He suspected her habit of rescuing outcasts was borne out of a want of love in her life. Not for the first time did he wish her marriage had burdened her with children of her own.

"So you brought another stray home with you? I really hoped you would grow out of that habit." He sighed. "What were you doing at the inn in the first place?"

"I was returning from a picnic with friends."

She looked up at him, her large eyes full of hope. "She is really very lovely. Kind. Not at all forward. Very quiet indeed."

"Quiet," the duke murmured reverently. "That must be refreshing."

"Oh, dear," Fanny consoled as she rubbed his arm. "Has Rebecca visited home recently?"

Nicolas had a handful of adult children, some of which had presented him with grandchildren too. Most of them were unruly, and the noise when they gathered together frequently sent him running for his library for peace and quiet. At the moment, he had left behind his second eldest daughter, Mrs. Rebecca Warner, at the family estate with his youngest daughter Jessica. Just thinking of going back to listen to them squabble made him long to stay in London far beyond his needs.

"She arrived last week and intends to stay another after my return," he said with a heavy sigh. "With a few of her closest friends in tow too," the duke complained.

"Oh, poor Jessica," Fanny said, wincing at her youngest sister's company for good reason. Rebecca's friends would put ideas in her head. Ideas and dreams he did not care to think about. "You should have brought Jessica with you to London."

His youngest daughter Jessica was not out

yet but had acted as mistress of the ducal country seat for a number of years. She was extremely capable, much to Rebecca's chagrin.

"Jessica wouldn't hear of coming with me and I much rather she stay at home until she comes out anyway. She's always happier in the country."

"You mean you're happier with Jessica in the country," Fanny chided sternly. "She's almost of an age to come out, Father. Next year she will have her season. You cannot keep Jessica a little girl for much longer."

"I can try," he promised, trying not to say it through gritted teeth.

Fanny gave him a look that suggested she saw through him. "The society around Stapleton is not diverse enough, and you know it," she chided. "She has to experience something of the world if she is to make the right choices for her future. She needs to meet young men too."

Nicolas believed himself a good father which meant no one was ever good enough to marry his daughters. He hadn't particularly liked Fanny's late husband, but he'd tolerated the match because Fanny had been smitten with the man.

He looked around the pretty room, ready to return to the topic of conversation that had brought him here in the first place. "So where is the governess you took in now? I trust you found her a better position than she had."

Fanny gave a guilty shrug. "We were upstairs before your knock at the door. Her name is Mrs. Gillian Thorpe, she's been widowed many an unhappy year."

The woman was still here? Damn, but he had hoped this was not another overstepping servant Nicolas might have to give their marching orders to. He was in quite the mood already and he'd use his title to protect his daughter today. "Well? Trot her out. Lets take a look at this supposed paragon of female virtue."

Fanny punched her hands to her hips. "She has not pulled the wool over my eyes, Papa."

"I'll be the judge of that," he insisted with a grim expression. "I won't tolerate any nonsense or delays this time round."

"Father! Quiet she might hear you," Fanny complained.

The last woman Fanny had taken in had stayed half a year before Nicolas had learned about her, accepting all manner of gifts from Fanny as if it were her right. Nicolas had found her a position four counties away with a family that rarely came to London but once a year.

"I hardly care for the sensibilities of a woman who would allow herself to be spoiled undeservedly. I knew the last one was trouble the first moment I met her," he said. "I will not allow you to be used again by anyone."

"All right, but remember to curb your tongue and be polite," Fanny pleaded. "She makes me laugh like no one else can. I like her very much."

"You like everyone at first sight," he grumbled, and they moved to the hall together. "It's only later that you notice their true colors and grasping ways."

Fanny rushed to get ahead of him. "She's this way."

A few steps along the hall Nicolas paused and head cocked to the side. A woman was complaining, quite loudly, to someone else.

"No! Absolutely not! Take them back," the woman cried.

There was a mumbled response he could not quite catch but suspected it was Fanny's maid speaking back to whoever it was.

"No! I don't care what Lady Rivers told you to do," the stranger continued. "Oh, give them here, and I will hang them back in her wardrobe myself."

"I thought you said she was quiet?" Nicolas hurried toward the voices immediately.

As he reached the hall near Fanny's bedchamber, he saw the stranger marching through the house. He stopped, bracing one arm against the wall as the scene between the woman and Fanny's ladies maid played out before him.

"She will not dismiss you over this you silly girl," the woman insisted, unaware of her audience, before marching into Fanny's bedchamber carrying a mountain of clothing. "I certainly don't need six more gowns," she insisted in a loud, clear voice. "I have enough as it is."

"But she said she never wears them. She said you would need them," Fanny's maid promised, chasing after.

Nicolas eased closer to hear the rest of the exchange.

"I don't care what she said I would want or not want," the woman argued. "A governess has no need for silks or velvet riding gowns. I'd rather go out without a stitch of clothing than accept so much charity from anyone."

Nicolas choked on a laugh.

The woman suddenly reappeared from Fanny's bedchamber doorway and spotted him in the hall. Her eyes widened. "Oh!"

"Hello," Nicolas began, moving toward the argumentative woman. "What happens here?"

The woman scowled. "I am trying to return the gowns Lady Rivers keeps foisting upon me."

"Foisting?" Nicolas stalked closer to the woman until he towered over her. He was comfortable intimidating people with his greater height. One look up at him and those in the wrong tended to stammer.

"Yes, foist." A merry smile appeared on her face though as she stared up at him without fear or apparent concern. "I do like that word, don't you? It makes me think of the season and all those unwise choices debutants will make."

"It is one of my favorite words." His hand shot out before he could stop himself. "You must be Mrs. Thorpe."

"I guess I must be. How do you do?" They shook hands, and much to his shock he lingered over her until she pulled her hand back. He was never usually so friendly to governesses, especially pretty unemployed ones.

Mrs. Thorpe, however, saw nothing forward in his behavior and beamed a brilliant smile his way. "And you are?"

"Nicolas Westfall."

Her eyes narrowed upon him and then she peeked at Fanny. "Is this another friend of yours that I simply *must* meet?"

Nicolas laughed outright. It was a novelty to be seen as something other than *Father* or *the Duke of Stapleton*. Anonymity was rare around members of his family. "Something like that."

Fanny rushed forward, and her next words spoiled the moment for him. "Gillian Thorpe may I present my father, the Duke of Stapleton."

"Oh. Oh, I see." The woman stared at him and then drew back a step, no doubt aware of her position in the world and of his greater one too. He was amused that she did not immediately curtsy to him. Instead, she punched her hands to her hips and kept her gaze on him. "Can you be counted on to stop Lady Rivers giving me things I do not need?"

Nicolas laughed, pleased that the mention of his title hadn't turned the woman into a simpering flirt as often happened. "I have tried to curb her generosity to no avail all her life. If she is not giving things away, she is bringing strays home with her. She is determined to look after everyone. She's been that way since childhood, only then she brought home wounded birds and lost dogs. Lately, it has been strangers eating at her table. Most people simply give in and accept rather than fight with her."

"I am not most people, your grace." Mrs. Thorpe colored suddenly and then dipped an elegant curtsy to him finally, and then faced Fanny with a determined expression. "You have to promise to stop this nonsense, or I will leave tonight."

Nicolas grinned at the steel in her voice. This was not a woman who planned to make use of Fanny's money. He couldn't help but like her for standing her ground.

Fanny suddenly held up her hands in surrender. "You are the most stubborn of women."

Gillian Thorpe smiled widely. "That's a promise I expect you to keep, my lady. Excuse me."

She spun about and returned to a bedchamber but reappeared a moment later with a hatbox in hand. She thrust that at Fanny's nervous maid. "I do not wish to see this hatbox ever again," she told the girl firmly. "Or the contents."

Nicolas shook his head. What a governess she must have made. No wonder Lady Lowell wanted to be rid of her. In a household run by women, there could only be one woman in charge. He could easily imagine this woman defending her charges from suitors and false friends, and their own mothers, too, if necessary. Jessica, motherless for most of her life, needed such a woman in her life. "I see now that gossip is woefully misinformed about the nature of your relationship."

"Of course it is wrong," Fanny said at the same time as Mrs. Thorpe. "We are the best of friends," Fanny continued.

Mrs. Thorpe colored a little at Fanny's remark and shook her head. "Your daughter is the kindest person I've ever met, your grace. I am very grateful for her intervention and offer of shelter until I can find a new position as a governess, but I do wish she could be less generous with strays."

Nicolas wholeheartedly agreed. Mrs. Thorpe was a confidant woman, and he admired that quality very much. She had a delightfully direct way of speaking too. "I've wished for that too."

Fanny touched his arm suddenly, pulling his attention from the governess. "Will you stay for luncheon?"

He hadn't planned to stay, but as he snuck another glance at Mrs. Thorpe, he decided he should. His youngest daughter was in need of a new governess. This one seemed almost ideal. Mrs. Thorpe might just be stubborn enough to withstand his family if she was known to have his complete support in all things related to Jessica. "I believe I'd enjoy that very much if Mrs. Thorpe would consent to join us too."

He saw Mrs. Thorpe's refusal even before she began to shake her head.

He would not be denied today. "Fanny mentioned you were a governess and a good one I suspect. Before that a wife with an undoubtedly happy husband. My youngest daughter is expected to come out next year and I'd like to help avoid those unwise choices you mentioned."

Her lips parted but no sound came out.

Despite the silence, he was pleased she hadn't said no immediately because he was about to be somewhat indelicate. "A woman like you, so confident, so sure of yourself could only have had a happy and satisfying marriage."

"Father!" Fanny protested.

"No, this is too important not to say upfront. Mrs. Thorpe, your husband was undoubtedly fortunate in his choice of bride. There are many things I cannot speak to my youngest daughter about concerning marriage, my other daughters live elsewhere, and I am certain Jessica will have bold questions to ask of another lady who has been through the experience of matrimony and the marriage bed. She cannot wait upon the mail from her sisters for her answers."

Mrs. Thorpe grew pale. "I see."

"It is none of my business what you talk about, and we will never need to speak of this again but I will expect you to answer Jessica's questions honestly, no matter how scandalous they might be."

She licked her lips, eyes downcast. "I could do that," she whispered.

Mrs. Thorpe kept her eyes lowered and he sighed at she'd turned shy. Undoubtedly, he was in the wrong, but he was asking the exact same questions he'd planned to ask other governesses in interviews tomorrow.

Given the last governess' pathetic advice to Jessica—repeatedly asking her to keep her knees firmly pressed together around any male she met—Nicolas felt he had no choice but to conduct interviews personally. "Having once had a wife and daughters to raise without her, I know women talk about things I shouldn't ever be privy to. Excellent. I'm glad that is settled."

"Nothing is settled, your grace," Mrs. Thorpe said suddenly, looking up at him with unexpected anger. "I have not said I wanted the governess position you offer."

Fanny laughed heartily. "Do you see what I mean about her making me laugh?"

Fanny assumed Mrs. Thorpe was joking, but Nicolas knew better. He had uncovered a very strong-minded woman, which made him all the more determined to employ her. "I do not offer you a governess position. I want you for Jessica's companion."

"Companion?"

He nodded, enjoying her surprise and the interest in her eyes. "I think you are just the sort of woman my daughter needs to consort with if she's to make the right choices in her life. Jessica is already strong-willed and determined. All my children are, unfortunately. I need someone who is not afraid to stand up to them and make them listen. I think you and I could manage Jessica very well together."

Mrs. Thorpe regarded him a long moment, clearly tempted. "Only time will tell if we can get along, your grace."

He beamed at her. He liked that she didn't

leap in to agree with him. Too many women did that already. "I do like your attitude, madam. Please, won't you join us for luncheon so we might become better acquainted."

She returned his smile and nodded. "All right, but only if you promise to let Lady Jessica decide if she wants me for her companion."

"Deal. We will leave London as soon as you are packed and then you can meet Jessica." He held out his hand again. "Do you have any tips for a poor father so he may steal a few minutes peace each day?"

Mrs. Thorpe took a step toward him, gripped his hand firmly and said in all seriousness. "You could always lock the doors as I've had to do around Lady Rivers."

He laughed even as Fanny complained that was unfair. Damn, but Fanny had been right—Mrs. Thorpe made him laugh, too.

Chapter One

———•———

Nine months later,
Stapleton Manor

Nicolas loathed the excesses of the festive season. His estate, his very home, was awash in lively chatter and the ever-present threat of standing beneath a maliciously placed clump of mistletoe.

Nicolas was far too old for such nonsense at four and forty years, and if he did kiss anyone, he certainly wouldn't advertise the fact in a public display of affection.

That was why he suppressed an oath as Miss Natalia Hawthorne's eyes flashed as she moved closer. Sensing danger, he glanced up, noted he was near another clump, and hastily took a pace back. His neighbor's daughter was far too young to be chasing after him. She was only eighteen, a year older than his youngest daughter, for God's sake.

Miss Hawthorne pouted. "La, your grace. You are a tease."

He was not. What he *was* feeling was entirely murderous toward the woman who'd formed the guest list and included such a flirt in their number. He should never have opened his home to guests for this farce, a weeklong Christmas party to prepare his youngest child, Jessica, for her coming out during the upcoming summer. Nicolas had felt this a bad idea from the very beginning and discovered so at every turn. However, his daughter had pushed, and even Jessica's companion had agreed a party that included family would be beneficial.

Since the companion and this particular daughter rarely agreed on anything concerning Jessica, he'd put up a weak protest then crumbled.

What he had not expected was to be hunted as if he were a prize on the marriage mart, too.

He retreated to the library, his private refuge, for protection. A haven for gentlemen—greenery and female free—the library was already occupied by a neighbor with the same idea as he. He scowled at Gideon

Whitfield, a longtime friend and confidant. "I wondered where you'd disappeared to."

"Do they have you on the defensive again, too?" Whitfield queried from where he sat, making himself at home with his feet stretched out toward the crackling fire. Whitfield, a gentleman in his prime, was a confirmed bachelor of retiring habits, fortunate enough to still have a full head of dark wavy hair that the ladies so often admired.

"Indeed." Nicolas took a peek outside toward the snowy drive. The dark of night was not far off, but he was expecting carolers to arrive at any moment. "Why did I agree to this?"

"Because you would do anything for your daughter's happiness." The man leaned forward. "You know, if you chose your own wife, you might be spared the worst of female machinations during the coming season. Like wolves, women only chase if you run. Let one catch you and your cares will be over."

He grunted. That was another reason he was dreading the upcoming season. As much as he'd enjoy the idea of taking a wife again, to have sex and companionship and even more sex, he could not consider it until his daughter had found a suitable husband. Only one of them needed to be on the marriage mart, and at his age, he had trouble imagining starting over.

It had been just he and Jessica for a number

of years, except for a string of governesses who had come and gone for various reasons. Earlier this year, he'd employed a companion for Jessica instead of a governess and been very pleased with the results.

Mrs. Gillian Thorpe had from the start been the exception to an otherwise unexceptional string of females he'd hired to keep Jessica in line. Mrs. Thorpe made no attempt to manage anyone but Jessica, and ensured he was always informed about disturbances to his daughter's routine. He currently had the perfect arrangement and was in dread of the next large change in his life—losing Jessica to a husband who had better deserve her or else.

"That is why you are here," he told Whitfield, pushing aside his unease. "Since my sons are otherwise engaged, you alone must distract females in want of a husband with your prettier face and deep pockets."

Nicolas was indeed no prize to look at, with his broken nose and hair showing more gray than the black he'd been born with. There were times Nicolas felt positively ancient beside Whitfield, who was nearly a decade his junior. But for all the years between them, they had a great deal in common.

Besides, of all his friends, Whitfield was entirely to be trusted around his innocent youngest daughter.

Whitfield waggled his eyebrows. "Oh, but you're the duke every woman wants to catch, or so your daughter's claim, even with your annual sour Christmas disposition on full display."

"Please don't remind me of the season."

"I am cruelly used as your shield," Whitfield complained, but amusement colored his tone, leaving Nicolas in no doubt that he was happy with his role in this particular house party. Whitfield leaned his head back. "Promise you've placed me next to someone other than the companion for dinner?" Whitfield begged.

Whitfield's hopeful expression brought a laugh bubbling out of Nicolas' chest. The younger man's pretense of being a put-upon bachelor amused him. The fool relished his current popularity among the fairer sex. "I had a word with the housekeeper, and she assures me the place settings will not change again. You are placed next to Jessica this evening."

"Good," Whitfield said, smiling broadly. "No offense intended to your charming companion, but all she ever does is talk about her charge. I may as well sit beside Jessica at least one night and hear of her adventures firsthand. Tell me though, do all of your servants have no other information to share other than what Jessica did last?"

"Mrs. Thorpe is devoted to my daughter," he said with satisfaction. "They are always together, so it is not surprising she speaks of Jessica a great deal. I couldn't have asked for a better woman to guide her at this age."

"Jessica seems to have slowed down very little since I last saw her," Whitfield mused. "Two months ago, she was still the cheeky hoyden who almost took my head off playing cricket and then laughed about the near miss I had."

"You do play exceptionally badly. You're supposed to catch the ball with your hands, not your head," Nicolas joked, remembering that sunny day fondly. Even Mrs. Thorpe had been laughing so hard she'd complained of a stitch in her side. Nicolas had had to chase after the furious Whitfield to make sure his daughter wasn't strangled or dumped in the nearby pond.

He took another peek outside and was pleased to see approaching carriages. "Here they come. We should gather my guests and go out to meet them."

Unfortunately, the fast clip of footsteps warned Nicolas his sanctuary had been invaded by a woman, and greeting the carolers might have to wait a little longer.

"I must speak to you about Jessica, Father," Nicolas' daughter, Mrs. Rebecca Warner, exclaimed abruptly.

He turned slowly, doomed to yet another inevitable lecture about the right way to raise a female child. Rebecca was forever telling Nicolas what to do, as if he'd not managed to turn out two satisfactory female children before. Rebecca took her role an elder sister to extremes.

She turned her attention on Whitfield and smiled at the man. "Do excuse us."

"No, stay exactly where you are." Nicolas wasn't about to have his evening spoiled by having his friend shooed away by the family's feminine major general. "Whatever you have to say can wait until tomorrow, Rebecca."

Whitfield fled anyway.

Wretched coward.

"You cannot put me off forever," Rebecca insisted, as she looked about the space with a critical eye. "This room could do with a good airing. Some flowers, perhaps, too."

Nicolas shuddered. Flowers and women were unwanted in this room, and his oldest daughter knew his wishes but still persisted in trying to change things. Perhaps there was merit in considering taking a wife who might just do things his way once in a while.

He smiled, wishing he could forbid his daughter from bothering him about a matter he had well in hand, but however opinionated Rebecca might have become, she was still family. Family mattered to Nicolas very much. "The carolers are coming up from the village. We must greet them."

"Wait just a moment," she cried out.

Nicolas strode away, called his guests to order, and announced the impending arrival of the carol singers.

Jessica rushed toward him, already rugged up against the cold and clearly excited. "Oh, I love Christmas, Papa."

"I know, Little Mouse." He threw his arm around Jessica's shoulders, hugged her to his side, and then looked for Mrs. Thorpe.

The raven-haired companion was still some distance away but already smothered in coat, gloves, woolen scarf and knitted cap until only a little of her face could be seen. "Shall we?"

He earned a tiny smile from Thorpe, who remained at his side as they strode out into the cold along with his family and guests. The steps soon filled to overflowing.

As they waited for the carolers to begin, he felt an absence and glanced around. Mrs. Thorpe had stopped a few paces behind him. He gestured her forward to stand beside Jessica. "You won't see a thing loitering there."

"I would be happy just to listen, your grace," she said with a shake of her head.

"Nonsense." He placed his hand on her back and positioned her to his right, just before him. "There now. You can see everything with Jessica far better from here."

She shivered, glancing over her shoulder to where his hand remained on her coat.

"My apologies." Nicolas quickly put his hands behind his back, slightly embarrassed. He did not ordinarily manhandle his female staff.

Mrs. Thorpe exchanged a quick smile with Jessica, and the pair huddled closer.

Nicolas let out a sigh of contentment. Mrs. Thorpe might just be the perfect companion. He'd felt it from he start. Quiet and kind, indulgent but not easily swayed by Jessica's impetuous habits. She was always ready to laugh at his poor jokes, too, and never put herself forward. In all the time he'd known her, before and after her employment in his household, she'd never once given him any encouragement. He had become curious about her past recently, though. After having her under his roof for so many months without incident, he'd grown comfortable around her as he was with few women.

Nicolas leaned forward. "How are you enjoying the evening?"

"This has been the perfect Christmas," Jessica promised, full of her usual enthusiasm for everything that had to do with making merry.

Mrs. Thorpe held her tongue. Nicolas softly nudged her with his elbow, in case she'd not realized the question was meant for her too. It was important to him that the woman in charge of his daughter was happy. "Mrs. Thorpe?"

"I… Oh, yes." Her eyes darted away, and a

frown turned down her lips in a brief but telling moment as she looked toward Rebecca. She smiled brightly. "I am having a wonderful time."

Now, what was this? A lie? Never in all the time she had been working for him had Mrs. Thorpe been anything less than forthright with her opinions. But the last time Rebecca had come to stay, he'd been aware of a little tension between the two women. He'd hoped the reason for that had passed. "Are you sure?"

"Absolutely," she assured him as the carolers began to sing.

Jessica leaned against him, and by dint of proximity, Mrs. Thorpe did too, to some degree. He held his daughter close to his chest, full of love for his last child, but was acutely aware that Mrs. Thorpe stood close and wasn't fully enjoying herself. He would talk to her about it after dinner and find out if his children had been meddling in their arrangement regarding Jessica's care again.

He shivered as a chilling breeze sprung up and snow swirled about them all. Nicolas could not afford to lose Mrs. Thorpe. Not when he needed her loyalty most.

Chapter Two

———•———

"Why do I have to sit in a stuffy room full of old people?" Lady Jessica exclaimed as she brushed aside the helping hands of her maid and flopped into a fireside chair.

Long used to such outbursts, Gillian Thorpe, the girl's companion of nearly nine months, hurried across the room to slip her finger under Jessica's chin and lift her gaze. "My dear, we discussed this. His grace agreed to host a house party so you might have more opportunities for making polite conversation before your season begins. Be reasonable. You know how much he dislikes Christmas. We must go back downstairs, even if it's only to wish everyone pleasant dreams."

The girl scoffed. "You mean I must exchange dull pleasantries that make my sister happy, too."

"Well, yes." Gillian winced. Mrs. Warner, Lord Stapleton's daughter, was extremely hard to please. For all that she was an infrequent visitor at the Stapleton estate, she behaved as if this was still her home and issued orders left and right. Often going against the duke's wishes, which was where trouble always sprung from between them. "She *is* your sister."

"You can have her," Jessica grumbled.

"I would have liked a sister, but I got a brother instead," Gillian told her.

"I didn't know that." Jessica's eyes lit up with curiosity. "What is he like? Where does he live?"

"I don't know, unfortunately. I lost touch with him when I married."

Her brother Lincoln and late husband Wallace Thorpe hadn't gotten along well, and she had always regretted that her letters had gone unanswered by her brother.

"But that's terrible," Jessica exclaimed. "We must find him."

"One day perhaps." Gillian sighed and then focused on the present—getting Jessica out of this room and in a happy mood. "But first, we must rejoin your family below."

The guest list for this rare Christmas weeklong party at Stapleton Manor had not hinted at an older generation when Gillian had been shown the names of those invited. She'd been hoping, as had Jessica, for a much younger crowd to engage with, along with the duke's family. Anyone below the age of their nearest neighbor, Mr. Gideon Whitfield, would have done.

But most of the duke's children, expecting their father's disinterest in the festive season, had made other plans and sent their regrets.

They had to make do with Mrs. Warner's friends instead. They would not have been Gillian's choice if she'd had any say in the matter.

It was Gillian's job to ensure Jessica was ready to make her come out, and the girl had proved as much of a challenge as her father had initially suggested when he'd offered her the position of companion nine months ago. Jessica took instruction well but seemed incapable of staying at arm's length from servants, which had become Mrs. Warner's chief complaint.

And it was true that Jessica was interested in the servants around her perhaps more than appropriate for a duke's daughter. She was as open and friendly as Lady Fanny Rivers, the duke's other daughter. There had been more than one evening when Jessica had sought her out late at night and ended up falling asleep in Gillian's own bed. The girl had never known her mother, and she often missed her older sisters dreadfully.

Yet making friends with the hired help was not what Jessica needed most. What she did need was an ally, a friend closer to her own age to share experiences with when in London. Gillian had been encouraging a friendship with one young woman in particular for that very purpose. "Miss Hawthorne is quite lively."

Miss Hawthorne was a year older than Jessica, had an excellent mind and, more importantly, was open to discussing the merits of one gentleman over another. That girl was aware of the appeal of men in a way Jessica had yet to discover for herself. Gillian was waiting for the right time to suggest the duke sponsor the girl for a London season too as her parents could not afford the expense.

"She wants my papa's attention," Jessica grumbled.

Gillian quickly dismissed the maid, afraid there was another tantrum in the wind. The Duke of Stapleton was a fine gentleman, both in looks and character. The duke had presence quite beyond what was normally found in men. He drew the eye, he made Gillian squirm with an impossible longing she did her best to fight. It was possible Miss Hawthorne had designs on becoming the next Duchess of Stapleton— possible, but very unlikely that such a wish might come to pass. From what Gillian could tell, her employer was actively trying to avoid the girl, and that was for the best. Miss Hawthorne wasn't right for him.

Yet one day, some lucky woman would catch Stapleton's eye and come between father and daughter forever. There would be a husband for Jessica and a second wife for the duke no doubt. The duke would need someone for company once Jessica began her new life. It was not meant to be part of her duties, but Gillian felt it was her unspoken duty to prepare the girl for such an eventuality. "If he finds a woman he likes, what is wrong with that?"

"He cannot marry someone my age," Jessica blurted out. "I absolutely forbid it."

Gillian chuckled softly. Lord Stapleton and his youngest daughter were both very particular. There had been a string of nurses and governesses before Gillian, and all had been dismissed after a few months of service for one reason or another, or so she'd been warned. Gillian had lasted nine months, something of a record here at Stapleton.

Gillian smoothed Jessica's hair behind her ear. While the bond that had formed between father and daughter gave Jessica all the love and security she could ever need, it had also created problems that Gillian was trying very hard to overcome in the gentlest way possible.

The girl was stubborn, prone to tantrums when thwarted. She had been indulged by all who knew her. Jessica could not accept anyone ever coming between herself and her beloved papa.

Although Gillian was patient and had tried to explain she might have to share his affections eventually, Jessica was so very young and had been terribly sheltered. She appeared rather naïve when it came to romantic relationships, too, and Gillian had come to the conclusion that Lord Stapleton had kept news of his amours far away from his daughter's ears.

But in their current situation, poised on the eve of Jessica's first season, tongues were wagging furiously about Stapleton's personal life. Jessica had heard how her papa was universally admired for his wealth and title. The talk annoyed Jessica. It scared the girl, too.

Gillian captured the girl's hand and squeezed. "You cannot stop your father from having his head turned and marrying if that is his heart's desire."

"I can and I will," Jessica promised, stubborn to the end.

Gillian adjusted the collar of Jessica's spencer, ensuring she was covered as much as possible. The halls and public rooms were often cold here at Stapleton, and the last thing His grace would want is his daughter presenting herself to the guests with a red, dripping nose. "How will you do that when you have a new husband yourself, claiming all of your time after your first season?"

For a moment, the girl appeared confused. "I... Well. I will. You will have to help me convince Papa to call the coming out off."

"I cannot do that. He hired me to make sure you'd be ready." Besides, Gillian had no intention of doing so. She knew how much the girl would yearn for a family of her own one day. "Come along. Your father's guests are waiting to see you."

"Oh, very well. I'd rather the way it used to be. Just the three of us, and Whitfield's visits now and then." The girl worried at her lip. "I suppose I must smile even when Lord James butts into our conversations like he always seems to do."

Lord James, second son of the Marquess of Newfield, was younger than Whitfield, and had from the outset gravitated toward Jessica. He was very friendly. Perhaps too marked in his interest for Gillian's tastes, on so short an acquaintance, but all men approached women in different ways.

As far as Gillian could tell, Jessica hadn't the slightest clue she was being pursued. That worried her. She would have to be blunt with the girl again. "Lord James admires you."

The girl blinked a few times. "Well, he can admire me all he likes when he's on the other side of the room. He does not have to be party to every conversation I have."

"He's trying to get to know you, my dear. I believe he likes you romantically. I think he might be courting you." The girl frowned. "Jessica, when a man likes you, he will find ways to make you notice him. Lord James likes to sit at your side, and his butting in is his way of making you look at him."

"I prefer the way other men court women. Papa sits beside you and never says a word."

Gillian laughed heartily. Jessica may not be aware of other men, but she noticed everything about her papa. "His grace sits beside me so he might avoid speaking altogether. He is certainly not courting me. After nine months of living here, he feels safe around me."

Jessica gaped. "That is so unromantic, and unfair of him to use you so ill."

"That is how it should be between us. Jessica, my dear, you forget again that your father employed me to take care of you, not him."

"Would you look after him if you could?"

Gillian gasped. "Jessica! Stop changing the subject."

The girl giggled. "Well, if we must talk about my suitors, we should also talk about you having one too."

"No. I'm much too old for marriage."

"You're only eight and twenty years old. You could have another husband, and a child to love. My father describes you as a fine woman, and he's never wrong."

"He did?" Gillian quickly shook aside a sudden burst of pleasure. Every woman, even an old widow like herself, could be forgiven for preening a little when complimented by someone of distinction. However, she ruthlessly refocused on her charge. "Tell me what you think of Lord James?"

"I like him well enough, I suppose?"

"One way to know if you might like him is if the idea of kissing him appeals to you."

Jessica scrunched up her nose. "Do I have to?"

"Most husbands will kiss their wives at some point in their marriage. It is an idea you must consider and accept," she warned. She wanted Jessica to choose well and have no regrets. Marrying for wealth, comfort, was all very well, but without love and mutual affection, it could seem an empty life indeed.

"They say Papa and Mama were always kissing."

Gillian felt a pang of envy. "And they were very happily married, were they not?"

"Would you kiss Papa?"

Gillian threw up her hands at the girl's foolishness. Lord Stapleton would never stoop to kissing a paid companion. "Stop your silly speculation about your father and I before you land me in a great deal of trouble. Companions have lost their positions, their very livelihoods, thanks to groundless accusations."

"I won't let anyone send you away over my nonsense." Jessica nibbled her thumb, then nodded slowly. "I really don't want to kiss Lord James, or anyone staying for the house party. I don't know if I'd want to kiss anyone, in fact."

Gillian winced. Hearing further verification that Jessica may not be ready for marriage gave her no pleasure. At Jessica's age, Gillian had discreetly experimented with kissing two local boys to know that she did want to do it again, but with someone better. Jessica might be well developed in her body, but she was far too young to recognize desire in others or in herself. Conversation appeared all she was interested in so far when it came to gentlemen.

Unfortunately, Mrs. Warner was not patient or understanding, forever pushing Jessica toward Lord James unless Gillian intervened. "Then you won't have to kiss him. Can we go down now before your father sends for us?"

"Oh, very well."

Gillian linked their arms and drew her toward the main staircase.

At this time of the evening, guests would be gathered in Stapleton's grand saloon one floor down. The duke had a lovely, comfortable home, except for the drafty halls and endless rooms to traverse to get anywhere. She would be very sorry to have to leave once Jessica was married, but there was no way around it. Once Jessica found a husband, Gillian had to find new employment.

Halfway down the stairs, Gillian glimpsed the first sign of trouble.

There was mistletoe attached to an unlit chandelier.

There was also the shadow of an unfamiliar figure lingering in the library doorway below. She had no idea who the fellow might be, but whoever it was could not be the right man to deliver Jessica's first kiss if he thought surprise was an option.

Her heartbeat quickened with concern. Gillian switched Jessica to her other arm so the girl could be maneuvered away from the man until his features became clearer. Jessica's first kiss would not be a mistake that might lead to an unwanted connection. This lurking stranger might be too interested in the size of Jessica's dowry rather than the girl herself.

Gillian discreetly peeked around as she remembered there was another way to get Jessica to the guests, a somewhat roundabout detour through the east wing and then down via the servants' stairs.

Making a snap decision, she jerked Jessica about—but walked straight into the hard body of a large gentleman.

She was caught, hauled close, and held tight against a very fine wool cloth coat. His scent was achingly familiar, and her body responded with unexpected pleasure. Gasping from the shock, Gillian glanced up into her employer's face, stunned that, even with the extra layers required for this drafty house, she could feel so much when he touched her.

Too much.

Stapleton frowned. "My apologies, Mrs. Thorpe. I should have been more careful."

He let her go slowly, making sure she was steady on her feet. Gillian darted a quick glance toward the shadows, but the lurking gentleman had fled. "It is entirely my fault, your grace. I should have been expecting you."

His brow lifted at her remark, a sight that made her insides quiver. He often held back his words, but his facial expressions fascinated her. She often watched him when she should be minding her own business, or Jessica's.

"I *was* wondering where you'd got to." He cleared his throat. "Both of you."

"A hem needed stitching." Gillian sighed as she fibbed about the reason for their absence. Informing the duke his daughter was trying to avoid the guests again would not make him happy.

"Oh, look," Jessica exclaimed suddenly. "You are both standing under mistletoe."

Gillian glanced up and stared in consternation at a second bunch that she had not noticed.

Lord Stapleton growled. "If I ever catch who keeps hanging this stuff about the place, I might just wring their bloody neck."

He yanked the offending greenery down, staring at it as if he might find the answers in the foliage.

"You have to kiss Mrs. Thorpe now, Papa," Jessica warned with a laugh.

"Jessica!" Gillian whispered in horror as she took a step back from the duke. Had nothing they'd spoken about earlier gotten through that girl's thick skull? She couldn't kiss the man who employed her. It was Jessica who needed to be romanced, not her father.

"I'm sure you'd like him to."

Silence descended, and for a moment, Jessica appeared stricken. She winced.

"I was sure I said that in my head," the girl whispered. "I'm so sorry."

The duke took a pace back, and the look on his face spoke volumes for his disgust at the idea of kissing a companion. Of kissing Gillian, in particular.

Properly embarrassed, Gillian caught

Jessica's elbow firmly and drew her down the stairs, hiding a sensation of crushing disappointment as best she could behind familiar tasks. "Come along Jessica, your sister will be wondering where you are."

Chapter Three

———•———

Nicolas stared after Mrs. Thorpe in utter shock. The idea of kissing him had surprised the widow, but that look on her face, acute disappointment, set his pulse soaring. However, he should not be kissing, or thinking of kissing, a woman who depended on him for her livelihood. He hoped she had missed his consideration of the idea.

"I must say, that was poorly done," Gideon Whitfield murmured as he stepped out of the shadows of the library.

Nicolas spun about, feeling guilty without having reason. "What?"

"You should have kissed her while you had the chance." Whitfield plucked the mistletoe from Nicolas' hand. "Might have been the only way to begin."

Nicolas clenched his jaw. "I am not interested in kissing."

"Liar." A fevered light glinted in Whitfield's eyes. "I've been watching you tiptoe around the woman for months. A good shag is just what you need. Admit it, you want her."

Disturbed by Whitfield's perception, Nicolas shook his head vigorously. If he did, he didn't mean to. "Don't be ridiculous. What are you doing lurking out here? I thought you had already gone home."

"A ruse." He pursed his lips, and then studied the clump of mistletoe. "I was trying to help a friend determine who is hanging mistletoe about the place. This is the fourth bunch I've seen today."

"And?"

"And nothing." Whitfield sighed. "No one else is around. Your guests are all still in the saloon as far as I can tell. I suspect it's just a bit of fun to pass the time for someone."

Nicolas gestured to the mistletoe. "I found three others this morning."

Whitfield whistled. "Perhaps its not for fun after all. Someone *is* determined to steal a kiss from someone."

"And desperate." Nicolas had his suspicions as to the culprit. Lord James' finances were not the best, and his estate could use a new injection of funds, not that Nicolas would agree to any match because Jessica hardly favored the fellow.

He scowled when Whitfield snapped his fingers. "I should be going."

How lucky was Whitfield to be a bachelor with a home close enough that he could leave? He had no one to answer to, and no one to notice his comings and goings or if he arrived safely. "Let me have a carriage brought out to take you home."

"No need." Whitfield stepped back into the library, wrapped his neck with a scarf, drew on his greatcoat and gloves and set a thick wool cap upon his head. "The short walk is always invigorating. I will be late tomorrow," he said as they reached the chilly entrance hall.

A covered lantern had been left on the hall table for his neighbor by a servant, so Nicolas lit it from a brace of candles and passed it over. "How late will you be?"

Whitfield shrugged. "Not sure. But I will certainly send word if I find I cannot make dinner."

Puzzled, Nicolas followed him to the door and let him out into the cold evening air. Whitfield had promised he had no other plans for this week and would be available every day and evening. If he were not present tomorrow, Nicolas would have to deal with the ladies on his own. A depressing thought indeed. "What are you doing over there?"

"I'll let you know after your house party ends," he said with a sly smile. "Try to enjoy what remains of your evening," he called as he strode away.

Nicolas shivered in the cold as he watched Whitfield plod along the garden path that led to his nearby home. He was tempted to follow him, just to avoid another hour of utter boredom. The only bright point in his evening was after Jessica said goodnight, he had just one further responsibility.

After his regular nightly conversation with Mrs. Thorpe, when they only ever talked about Jessica, he could finally go to bed and forget he had visitors.

Jessica greeted him at the saloon doorway and hugged him. "Good night."

"So soon, Little Mouse?"

Jessica nodded, hiding a yawn behind her hand. "I feel so very sleepy tonight."

She wandered off, Mrs. Thorpe trailing after her at a brisk pace.

He took a seat, but he knew from past experience that Mrs. Thorpe would return downstairs in precisely fifteen minutes. Punctuality was her stock in trade. She had done wonders for Jessica's tardiness by example. With luck, that habit would continue into her marriage.

The party broke up soon after and he bid all

good night and fled to his study, glad to have a few moments to collect his thoughts before his regular evening appointment.

He pulled Mrs. Thorpe's employment file from his desk drawer and studied it for the hundredth time. Gillian Thorpe intrigued him far more than she ever should. Nicolas had employed her the day he'd met her, mostly because he was impressed by her forthright nature and willingness to laugh.

Months of proximity and shared conversations had suggested she was very shy with gentlemen. She did not flirt but she seemed to like him. And she did not encourage anyone to think she might overstep her position. He knew very little about her life before she'd become a companion other than she'd been a wife once.

Mrs. Thorpe had smoothly become part of the household from the beginning, never forgetting that her only concern was Jessica's happiness. She rarely left the estate and he was glad. The idea he could lose Mrs. Thorpe went against his expectations. He could not do without her for Jessica's sake.

"Your grace?"

Mrs. Thorpe stood poised in the doorway with a shy smile on her lips.

Nicolas' heart beat a little faster. "Yes, do come in."

He quickly tucked her file away in his

drawer before she saw her name on the cover and schooled his features to give nothing of his thoughts away. One day Jessica would be gone, and so too would the unflappable Mrs. Thorpe.

"Jessica has had a wonderful day," Mrs. Thorpe began, moving quickly on to explaining in detail the ins and outs of their activities.

Mrs. Thorpe was always softly spoken, and he loved to hear her laugh. He admired her. He liked her. She had become important to Jessica, to him too. He would like to know her better. He *would* like to kiss her. She attracted him without even trying.

He shifted in his chair but found it difficult to retain a word she said tonight, because he could not stop wondering if he had made an error. For the past months, he believed these nightly meetings were to make sure of his daughter's happiness, never realizing he might just be stealing time to be alone with a companion for himself.

Gods, he was an old fool.

And a nervous one. He shifted to sit on the front edge of the desk as she continued on without a clue to what he was really thinking about her. He had to admit the more he watched her talk, the hungrier he became for a taste of her lips.

It was probably a mistake to wish, to hope, that he might not be rebuffed should he try to kiss her. It had been an eternity since his wife's death and years since he'd indulged in any sort of romantic affair. Fearing he was staring, he fumbled in his pocket for a handkerchief, and touched something else.

He withdrew his hand. "Devil take it!"

"Your grace?"

"Oh, um. Forgive me. It's *mistletoe*. Again." He stared at the cutting, wondering how and when he'd been gifted with this mischief-maker. "I…"

He looked at Gillian Thorpe. She had been the last person to stand close to him. She was the last woman to be in his arms in fact, aside from Jessica. The woman turned her face away, but he caught a glimpse of her cheeks reddening.

"If there is nothing else, I'll take my leave," she whispered.

Gillian Thorpe had planted mistletoe on him and was now too shy to go through with it.

"Actually," Nicolas said as he held the mistletoe over her head. If she wanted a Christmas kiss, who was he to say no? "There is one thing. Merry Christmas, Mrs. Thorpe."

He leaned forward slowly, giving the woman time to flee should she have changed her mind about kisses. When she simply stared at him, eyes wide, he closed the distance between them and pressed his lips to hers. He kissed her very softly, slowly nibbling until she sighed.

Gillian leaned into him, her hand rose to touch his jaw, and then she teased her finger into his hair.

Nicolas went up in flames.

He captured her face, drawing them dangerously close together. Their simple mistletoe kiss became so much more than he was ready for, so very quickly. He had his tongue in her mouth, his palms sliding toward her breasts, before he came to his senses.

He broke the kiss to apologize, panting hard. "Forgive me, Mrs. Thorpe. I have forgotten myself."

She stood slowly, gripped the back of her chair and, without looking at him, nodded. "Goodnight, your grace."

"Until tomorrow, Mrs. Thorpe."

It was not until she was gone that he could breathe properly.

Dear God. His cock was as hard as an iron spike from that one single kiss.

What the devil was he to do now? He did not really regret that kiss. It had been so long. He'd enjoyed it and believed, aside from a little embarrassment afterward, she had too.

He raked his fingers through his hair, uncertain of whether he needed to apologize or not. And now that he'd kissed her sweet lips, how was he supposed to resist wishing to do so again?

Chapter Four

———•———

Gillian peered outside, watching Jessica and Mrs. Warner walk the snowy gardens with Lord James. She was vastly annoyed. She had been duped into leaving the room, returning to discover Mrs. Warner had taken Jessica outside without inviting her to go along, too. The duke would not be pleased if she was negligent of her duties. Of course, Mrs. Warner was certainly a suitable chaperone, but Gillian believed her utterly biased toward Lord James' likely suit.

"Ah, there you are, Mrs. Thorpe," the Duke of Stapleton exclaimed.

"Good morning, your grace," she murmured trying not to blush.

He smiled softly as he drew near. "How fortunate I am to find you in this out of the way spot. Were you waiting for me?"

Gillian blushed deeply. She was outside his study door, so of course it might look that way to him. They had kissed after all. He might imagine she'd want to do so again.

Judging by the way he regarded at her now, he wasn't concerned she might be dangling after him. Which she wasn't. She desperately wished he would forget they had kissed. "I assure you it was not intentional. I wanted to see if the weather outside had cleared enough for a short walk. Oh look," she said quickly, "there is Mr. Whitfield at last, joining your daughters for a stroll about the grounds."

"I sent him out to put a stop to my daughter's rather transparent attempt at matchmaking," Stapleton promised as he brushed against her side. "Forgive me for teasing you today. I know you are the model of propriety."

"I do try, your grace."

Tried and failed last night—rather spectacularly, in fact. Gillian had not stopped thinking about her employer ever since their kiss, and in ways she was not supposed to consider him. It was very likely she could have shared his bed, if she'd not been scared witless by the very great risk she'd taken with her reputation.

He glanced behind them. "I shouldn't have kissed you last night."

She startled. "But you did. Why?"

He appeared puzzled. "I took advantage of you having put mistletoe in my pocket."

Her eyes widened as she realized what must have happened. Jessica must have put it in her father's pocket when she'd said good night to him! "I did not put mistletoe in your pocket."

Gillian put her hand over her lips. The kiss had been a mistake, and she'd pay for it somehow. "You must think the worst of me, but I know my place."

"Your place is exactly where you are." He studied her, and she grew warm under the intensity of his stare. "You did nothing wrong in my eyes."

"If you say so, but I am afraid others would disagree."

"Last night was all too brief to warrant any lasting awkwardness between us, but I do apologize if you were left unsatisfied. Your husband would have had much more leisure to do a better job of kissing you."

It took her a second to understand him, and then she blushed harder. She had let him believe she'd been happily married when they'd first met but the lie had come back to haunt her in the worst way. The truth was much too humiliating to share. "Oh, yes. Yes, he was very good at that."

He stared, and then his smile grew wider.

"I'm better."

She opened her mouth in shock. "No gentleman should ever say such a thing."

"Duke I may be, but have I ever claimed to be a saint, Mrs. Thorpe?"

Gillian shook her head. "I never imagined you were."

"Good." He swooped down and claimed her lips in a fierce kiss that took her breath away.

Gillian clung to him as her knees grew weak. Despite her previous experience with the duke, she was not prepared for this assault on her senses. His arms came around her, drawing her close. He kissed her soundly, drawing on her lips and shifting constantly against her body. Gillian lifted trembling arms around his shoulders as her legs threatened to buckle. Could any stolen kiss have ever been so thoroughly delivered before?

He drew back a little to speak. "You and I need a little privacy."

Although she shouldn't agree, she nodded anyway, feeling excited when he clasped her hand and tugged.

Gillian was led into his study, and the doors were closed and locked. Stapleton turned, captured her face, and proceeded to kiss her witless once more against the hard wood door. She found herself perched over his knees ten minutes later, his fingers in her hair, his lips tugging hers. She pinched herself, concerned she might be dreaming this.

She drew back. "Oh dear."

"So can I claim the distinction of kissing you better than your husband once did?"

"Oh, yes." She squirmed. He'd promised he hadn't wanted to know about her marriage. She'd never known such kisses existed. Wallace had certainly not kissed her like that. "Indeed, you have been quite thorough about it."

He laughed softly. "I had hoped it wouldn't be too hard to please you."

He kissed her cheek, and then her throat. Gillian shivered and clutched to him as he slowly lowered her backward onto the chaise they were sitting on.

As he hovered above her, Gillian panicked. She pushed him away and struggled to escape his clutching hands. "What have I done?"

One of the stipulations Lord Stapleton had insisted upon was that Gillian would share her knowledge of the delights of the marriage bed with Jessica, to prepare the girl. He had said he wanted Gillian to take her mother's place in explaining every facet of married life. Gillian had hedged about her experience quite a bit at that point, feeling acute embarrassment at the time. Gillian *had* been married, to a man twenty five years her senior, but she hadn't found her brief experience in the marriage bed at all delightful. Wallace had never kissed her with such passion.

She couldn't let Stapleton discover she wasn't as experienced as she'd promised him she was.

Her job depended on her maintaining propriety. She clung to the back of a chair for support. She was Jessica's companion, not his.

There was silence behind her for a great many minutes before Stapleton sighed heavily. "You've done nothing wrong, madam. I am entirely to blame yet again."

She was unable to look at him. She needed this position, and she could not leave Jessica to face her sister's machinations alone. "I quite understand. It was the mistletoe."

"And you." Stapleton approached and set his hands lightly on her shoulders. Even though she flinched, his hands remained steady on her skin. "Thank you very much for the kiss, Mrs. Thorpe. It was delightful, as is everything you do. Don't let me keep you any longer if you wish to go."

Chapter Five

———•———

Nicolas was unused to being frustrated by pretty widows. Usually they were desirous of his company and would never dream of turning away from his pursuit.

But this particular one was in his employ, and thus far proved a worthy adversary.

Gillian Thorpe was doing everything in her power to ensure the space between them was maintained. She'd deliberately stepped out of his path numerous times over the past two days and he was beyond amused by her new timidity.

If she did not want more kisses from him, fine. He would never pursue an unwilling woman. But he was concerned that she appeared quite embarrassed by what they had shared thus far.

Even if she'd been married and claimed to be experienced enough to guide Jessica, she was out of her depth when it came to the passion he'd discovered in their kiss.

That did not deter Nicolas from seeking her out at every turn, just for the pleasure of her calming company.

It was quite unlike him. He could not account for his interest or his desire that Gillian Thorpe should become as comfortable around him as she'd been before the first kiss. To that end, he'd scoured the house for the woman and, of course, found her in Jessica's shadow.

He slipped into the music room and shut the door quietly, knowing that his daughter's piano practice would cover the sound of his arrival.

His quarry was absorbed in the view out the window, but her fingers hovered over her lips.

He hoped she was thinking of his kisses because he dreamed of hers. Despite the rebuff, he still admired her very much.

And yet he couldn't afford to lose her from his employ.

Gillian Thorpe was essential—for his daughter's happiness and his own peace of mind.

Under Gillian Thorpe's watchful eye, Jessica was growing so confident in her abilities every day that he was relieved beyond measure at finding her. Jessica played beautifully, but her volatile temperament meant she took criticism to heart. When Jessica came out in society, her deportment would be under scrutiny from every quarter. A tantrum in public was quite out of the question.

The music stopped suddenly. "Papa."

Jessica flew across the room and into his arms.

Nicolas hugged her to him and kissed the top of her head, his heart full of love for the gift of his youngest child. It was moments like these he dreaded Jessica going away. She had grown up completely unaffected by her position in society. She had never held her title of lady over anyone of lower rank. She loved everyone equally depending only on the length of her acquaintance. "Good morning."

"Did you hear me play?"

"Indeed. It was so good, for a moment I swore it was Mrs. Thorpe at the instrument."

Gillian Thorpe played very well, but not often. She insisted that Jessica be given every opportunity for practice and adulation, so rarely played herself except if they found a difficult passage in the music that must be practiced.

"Oh, she still won't." Jessica tugged him toward the piano. "Convince her for me, Papa. Or better yet, play a duet with Gillian like you did once before."

He smiled, silently thanking fate for an excuse to linger. To sit at Gillian's side and rebuild her trust was imperative. "Will you do me the honor, Mrs. Thorpe?"

Her eyes darted toward the doorway, but she did nod. Nicolas waited for her to take a seat at the instrument then perched beside her on the narrow bench.

"What would you like to play, your grace?"

"Any lively tune will do." He smiled, but was far too aware of her proximity. "Last time I do not think I played very well. I should very much like another chance to impress you."

He was not only talking about the duet.

He wanted to kiss her again, so very much if she would give him another chance. If not, he wanted their easy companionship back.

But with his daughter present, unintentionally acting as their chaperone, the duet would have to do to begin with.

Gillian commenced to play, her fingers lightly tripping over the keys and producing the most wondrous of sensations in him. He had played the piece before, and found his place and began, playing against her lightness with his own music.

From the outset of their acquaintance, Nicolas had struggled not to read too much into their similarities. They both played the pianoforte exceptionally well, enjoyed the quiet, had similar tastes in books and, by all accounts, Gillian skated. Something he liked to do often when the lake froze over. Unfortunately, the weather had not yet been conducive to an outing until now.

"The head groundsman feels it safe to mount a skating expedition tomorrow," he murmured.

Jessica applauded then leaned against the instrument. "I cannot wait to show Gillian our special place."

He peeked at the companion, hoping to see interest. Mrs. Thorpe's fingers flew over the keys, but her lower lip was gripped between her teeth.

He leaned a little toward her. "Do say you will come skating with us."

"Yes, do come," Jessica said, beaming with excitement. "You said you skated every day as a girl. Maybe you have a better chance of keeping up with Papa than I do."

Gillian blushed. "I have long since lost my skill, but if I must fall down in public for your amusement, I surely will come with you."

"I would never let you fall," Nicolas promised, grinning from ear to ear. "Some experiences are not easily forgotten. A little practice and you'll be fine. Indeed, I am very eager to see if you are as competent a partner on the ice as your reference from Lady

Holsworthy suggested."

She blushed. "I'll do my best, your grace, but I am not to blame if Lady Holsworthy's praise far exceeded my actual skills."

"I've never been disappointed in you," he promised.

They finished the duet in silence, Nicolas aware that he was very eager for tomorrow. He too had spent many days flying around the ice on his own as a child. It was an escape, much like riding very fast, with only his own will powering his direction. He should like to see if he could impress Gillian.

She stood quickly when they reached the end of the piece. "If you would excuse us, your grace. Mrs. Warner and Mrs. Hawthorne are expecting Jessica at any moment in the drawing room."

"A moment," Nicolas said to delay her flight. Since Jessica had already turned for the door, he pitched his voice low. "You did not make our standing appointment last night. I was sorry to have missed speaking with you about my daughter."

She lowered her face. "I apologize, your grace. Jessica and I talked very late."

He studied her face, unsure if that was the truth or not. He didn't want to push her into his company, but he'd have to eventually. He relied on Mrs. Thorpe to keep him apprised of

Jessica's moods and whims. He could not have her avoiding him out of fear. "I would like to speak to you in private this morning then."

"Of course." She appeared nervous but nodded. "Let me escort Jessica, and then I will return in half an hour."

"To my study, if you please." Nicolas turned away, pulse jumping with nervousness and excitement. Avoiding each other could become tedious. They could not go on this way. "I'll be waiting."

Chapter Six

———•———

Gillian's heart beat wildly as she stood alone in Stapleton's quiet study, toying with the braiding on one of the two visitors' chairs placed before his desk. She had always spoken to her employer at night, long after his inquisitive daughter had retired to her bed, and she felt incredibly guilty for failing to meet with him last night. She'd been afraid to come lest he test her resolve to ignore his appeal.

She still wasn't sure she could. Ignoring Stapleton had been difficult enough seated beside him on the pianoforte, even with Jessica in the room. She knew what he wanted when he smiled at her so warmly. More kisses and other things.

Gillian was afraid and a fool. She might not be able to deny him when she wanted to be held in his arms again. It had been wrong but heavenly. She hoped she could get through this meeting without stammering or blushing.

"Forgive me for not being here when you arrived, Mrs. Thorpe," Stapleton began as he strode into the room. "Guests chatter incessantly. Please sit."

Gillian sank into a chair opposite his desk, expecting, hoping, he'd sit in his usual place behind it so she could calm her racing heart.

He chose the other chair, the one at her side before the desk, but clenched his hands together between his spread knees. His face was so serious that she felt weak with dread. "I wonder if I owe you an apology," he whispered.

She swallowed. "For what?"

"I don't ordinarily respond to dares, but for my behavior, I can offer no other explanation or excuse. It is embarrassing to me now that you might have felt pressured to let me have my way."

His apology pained her because it was so unnecessary. "I could easily have stopped you."

He stared, and then a corner of his lips lifted in a slow smile. "And you did quite the opposite."

Gillian frowned, turning away from him a little. "What does that say about me?"

"What does that say about us both? We were two people kissing."

"Indeed."

"And quite well, too, I must say." He laughed softly, and the familiar sound put her at ease. "So well it seemed to me we had kissed each other before."

Was he attempting to tease her? She stared at him, at his hesitant smile. "But we most certainly have never done so, or thought about it."

"Until now." His eyes glowed with a new warmth when he looked at her. "Perhaps it felt so easy since we have been acquainted for so long."

"A mere nine months since we first met at your daughter Fanny's house, and since my employment here began, most of those days and weeks were spent with your daughter between us," she whispered, feeling as hot and bothered as when his lips had been pressed to hers.

He pursed his lips, and then grinned. "Jessica has made an excellent chaperone up until now, wouldn't you say?"

"Usually, yes." Gillian glanced at him, wondering what he thought of her. "You owe me no apology, your grace," she assured him. "I am not offended, if you were not by my forwardness in allowing it."

"I thought your kiss sweet. Very exciting. I have not been able to stop thinking of you in my arms, and I do apologize if that admission makes you uncomfortable."

She met his gaze and saw the uncertainty she felt in his eyes, too. "I've not been able to stop thinking about you, either."

He grinned. "What shall we do about it? Jessica is not here. It is just us two alone in a private room. Two widows with no other romantic entanglements to get in the way. Should we explore this or go back to how things used to be?"

"You want me to decide?" Gillian's pulsed raced that he would give her a choice. However, it wasn't a fair question. She knew she wanted him. They were in a room with three chairs, a desk, and chaise and a fireplace rug. Was there a way for a man and woman to comfortably make love in such a setting? She became warm from just thinking about the possibility. "Is it private enough?"

"The staff are busy elsewhere, and my guests are occupied on the other side of the house with Jessica and Rebecca," he whispered huskily. "I made sure there were no idlers in the hall as I came in to speak to you."

Gillian glanced at him sharply. "So you have plans for me?"

"No plans." The quick smile he flashed made him seem so much younger than he was. "But should you have felt the need to scold me for my earlier impertinence, I wanted to be sure no one else would hear about it."

"Impertinence?"

He bit his lower lip and winced. "Flirtatiousness?"

Blinding heat covered her skin. "That kiss went far beyond flirtatious, your grace."

"Nicolas," he suggested. "If you don't object to me saying so, I'd like to kiss you like that again right now."

Her heart skipped a beat. *Nicolas.* His very name sent a thrill through her. Her pulse raced. He was offering her a chance to be his lover or turn him aside if the idea displeased her. Gillian wanted him, but she was afraid of how things might change if she admitted it.

"Perhaps we should discuss my daughter now," he said as his smile dimmed. "Tell me of yesterday, as you always do."

He leaned back casually and crossed his legs at the ankle. The pose suggested he was in no rush to resume *flirting* with her anytime soon.

Gillian gathered her wits. "Jessica enjoyed herself very much. Early that morning we walked along the lane for exercise with Lord James, and had Mr. Whitfield join us for the return trip. After luncheon, a lively game of charades was played, and although Lord James tried very hard, it was Mr. Whitfield who won the day, guessing most of Jessica's characters."

"She hasn't been able to fool him since she was nine," the duke said dryly, following it with a rare soft chuckle that caused gooseflesh to rise all over her skin. Stapleton had the warmest laugh of anyone she knew. The sound drew her closer, but she was always wary of overstepping with her personal opinion that Whitfield had more than a passing interest in her charge.

"They do seem well matched."

Stapleton merely smiled. "And after dinner, what topic was discussed most amongst the ladies?"

"The coming season." She watched his face carefully now. "Gowns, entertainments, dressmakers—bachelors in want of a wife."

As she'd anticipated, Lord Stapleton physically withdrew. As much as he might express his enthusiasm over his daughter's coming out with everyone else, in private with Gillian, she'd noticed he was less than enthusiastic about the idea. Neither father nor daughter seemed ready for the specter of looming separation a marriage would bring.

"I suppose Mrs. Warner led that discussion."

"She did, but Mrs. Hawthorne held her ground on the subject of necklines during a first season."

"Necklines?"

Gillian waved her hand before her chest.

"How much cleavage a young woman should show to avoid appearing fast in her first season."

"Is that the usual sort of conversation you must endure every night?" He winced. "It is times like this I despair of being a man."

"Why is that?"

"As a man, I enjoy a lower neckline. But as a father, I feel quite the opposite."

Gillian chuckled, and then realized that despite kissing Stapleton, they were still the same people. There was no awkwardness between them anymore. "I am certain most fathers grapple with that dilemma."

"What is your advice, Mrs. Thorpe?"

"For necklines? That you leave those decisions to her current dressmaker. The woman has excellent taste."

"No doubt you are right, as you have been in so many things." His smile returned. "Well, if there is nothing else, I should not keep you."

He stood, and held out his hand to assist her up, something he'd never done before. When Gillian slipped her palm over his, he gripped her hand gently. She could leave, and he would not mind that she'd denied him.

Or she could stay and discover if he did everything as well as he kissed.

She stood and kept hold of his hand, but her heart thudded loudly in her ears.

Nicolas paused, and then dipped his head slowly toward hers. Their lips brushed, a fleeting touch, but it was enough to light a fire inside her. Gillian slid her hands up his forearms until he embraced her.

"Ah, Gillian," he whispered between kisses. "You honor me."

Gillian wound her arms about his neck and gave herself up to Nicolas' passion. His grip was strong around her body, his hands slow in exploring her curves. She could not get close enough, and when his lips left hers, and his breath came hot against her throat, she moaned.

"Shh," he whispered. But his kisses grew bolder, the flick of his tongue teasing into her mouth more insistent, until Gillian could barely hold two thoughts together.

His hands cupped her breasts, and she gasped as he removed her shawl.

He lowered her into a chair gently and knelt before her on the rug. Then he buried his face between her breasts. "Necklines," he whispered, then laughed as he grasped her gown at the shoulders and tugged gently to lower hers.

His breath was hot and panting against the upper swells of her breasts. Gillian curled her fingers into his hair as he revealed one nipple. When he blew over the rosy peak, she almost launched herself into him. Wallace had only ever held them in his dry hands, and only in their bed at night. She was already well out of her depth with Nicolas but loving every moment.

"Patience," he whispered just before he took her nipple into his mouth. When he sucked, she swallowed a moan, astonished with how utterly good it felt to be made love to.

Nicolas made her wish that her marriage had been different. Her husband had merely lifted her night clothes, and quickly thrust into her a few times before groaning and rolling off to fall asleep immediately after. Her whole experience of the marriage bed had lasted mere minutes each time.

Seventeen times, to be precise.

She would not mind *Nicolas'* haste. She wasn't a wife but a lover, and as impatient as Nicolas appeared to be, too. She assisted him in removing his coat when he began to struggle out of it but became trapped by the tight sleeves.

Once he was free, Gillian grasped his shoulders again as he sank lower. His lips were on her knee, his hands skimming her thighs when sanity briefly returned. "The door."

"Locked." He pulled her forward until she perched at the very edge of the chair. His fingers teased between her legs until she was gasping in shock and anticipation.

Nicolas bit his lip again before murmuring, "Do you mind if I indulge you first?"

Gillian shook her head quickly without really knowing what he was suggesting. He could touch her anywhere he wanted, or she'd have to imagine him doing so later when she was alone in her room.

His head dropped, and his lips caressed her inner thighs, and then...

"Sweet mercy," she whispered as he lapped at her sex with his tongue.

He pushed her legs wider, until she was completely open and exposed to him. Despite the shock, it was wonderful. *He* was wonderful. A rush of pure sensation and wickedness filled her body and made her squirm. Gillian watched Nicolas taste and tease her through hooded eyes, never daring to close them completely in case he stopped.

But what he did to her was incredible. She felt too large for her skin, too far away from his. She pulled on him just as he did something that drove her body wild. She thrashed and cried out, muffling her mouth with her arm.

Gasping for breath, she collapsed back in the chair, boneless and overwhelmed by the Duke of Stapleton's lovemaking.

Nicolas held Gillian's legs up at the knees, and she felt no shame in that. She had never enjoyed intimacy until now. She'd also never known what her marriage had lacked before.

Releasing one leg, Nicolas unbuttoned his trousers, tucked his shirt up beneath his brocade waistcoat, and then slowly pressed inside her.

It took her overly sensitive body a moment to adjust, and then she reveled in his powerful thrusts, in his tight grip on her thighs, and the bright, lust-filled expression in his beautiful eyes as he took his pleasure.

This was not the duty she'd endured for her husband. This was something else, beyond her experience.

He caught her head and held her cheek in his palm when he finally slowed. He grinned. "So very good and easy. Are you sure we've not lain together before?"

Gillian took the question as it was meant— as a jest to prolong his passion. She laughed softly, and brushed her lips against his palm. "I would have remembered how very good you were if that were true."

He grinned, closed his eyes and exhaled, as if he were in heaven making love to her. He found a new rhythm, hard enough to move her backward with each stroke, deep enough that her own desire was suddenly rekindled.

She stretched to touch his face, craving more from him. "So very good, Nicolas."

He must have seen something in her

expression, for he touched her quim once more, teasing the little bud at the apex of her slit with skill and persistence. "Again?"

Gillian twisted her hips, gaining new sensations from the slight change of position. Exciting ones that would bring her to that moment of intense pleasure again. How did he do that when her own husband had left her feeling only empty and sore? "Yes, I think so!"

They drew closer, grinding together. She held his gaze, and then her body curled in upon itself, and she soared again, crying out in surprise the next moment.

Nicolas caught her cry with his mouth and stayed with her until she calmed.

He drew back his hips suddenly, then his hands left her skin. "Gillian," he gasped, panting hard as he spilled his seed away from her.

She remained as he had left her, and then slowly lowered her feet to sit up gingerly. For a change, there was no discomfort but a pleasant ache where this man had been joined to her.

Nicolas turned aside, straightened himself, then sat back on his heels. "Now we've done it."

She grinned, basking in his warm smile and presence. She should feel guilty, wanton, decidedly wicked. But she felt none of those, only pleased with herself for being brave. "We have. And very well done it was, too."

He swooped in to kiss her quickly. "A pleasure."

Gillian cupped his face a moment, feelings she should not experience growing for the man holding her. However talented he was in the arts of the bedroom, it was imperative that she not mistake this moment. He was a duke and she the paid companion. They could have no future together besides the carnal. It was just lust and loneliness drawing them together. "If there is nothing else, your grace, I should return to my duties."

He nodded, his grin dimming. "So we will say nothing of this?"

"Indeed. It will be our secret forever."

He stood, groaning and rubbing at his knees. But he held out his hand to help her up, repeating the moment that had led them into their dalliance. Gillian was grateful for his support and clung to his hand a moment longer than strictly necessary. Her legs felt decidedly weak. It had been a very long time since she had lain with her husband, never mind having found pleasure in the experience—climaxing twice in so short a span of time appeared to be an exhausting experience.

He lifted her hand to his lips and kissed the back of her fingers. "Until this evening."

"Yes."

Nicolas turned her hand over and kissed her

palm softly. Gillian's body quivered anew as he glanced up and licked across her palm. There was a devilish look in his eyes that she couldn't resist. Would they talk tonight or would he want to make love again? Once tasted, Gillian was certain she couldn't refuse a second invitation to pleasure.

She brushed her body against his deliberately as they parted, reveling in his warm, tortured groan. He swatted her backside lightly and she laughed with him, feeling the happiest she'd ever felt in her life. She could spend another sinful interlude in his arms. In fact, she was most eager for it. She blew him a kiss and sauntered out, feeling very good about herself, and beautiful too.

Chapter Seven

———•———

Everyone would say he should be ashamed of himself. Seducing the paid companion. Making love to her on a chair, in the broad daylight no less.

Nicolas hid his grin behind his scarf as he inspected the frozen lake bordering his property with his steward. It was a good day, and he was quite proud of himself. He was happy. "Are you sure it is safe?"

His steward, Fenton, had grown up on the estate and could be trusted to know if they should skate or not. "You'll all be fine as long as you don't host a ball out there."

"No chance of that." Ten skaters hardly made for a ball, and most likely few would gather together in one place or for long. Nicolas judged the outing could go ahead and gestured to his guests that they could begin.

Jessica and Whitfield were first out and made a quick circle around each other before being joined by the slower Miss Hawthorne and Lord James.

Nicolas found rum in a hamper and held it out. "To warm your heart on a cold day."

"My thanks, your grace." The man took a swift pull. "Colder than a widow's tit out here."

The remark made him think of Gillian, whose tits were hardly cold when they were under his lips. He glanced her way and noted how slow she was in buckling her skates. He felt a touch of urgency to see her on the ice and have her on his arm.

"A fair one, she is," Fenton remarked. "Outlasted the others by a wide margin. Cost me a pretty penny, too."

Fenton was a bit older than Nicolas, had never married, but had many ill opinions of the fairer sex he was always keen to share.

"Were you betting on the length of a servant's employment again?"

"It's only ever worth betting on the female ones." Fenton shrugged. "Hasn't been that much excitement about this year though. A man has to do something with his idle thoughts."

"Well, a word of advice. Don't bet against her again."

"That way, is it?" Fenton's mouth twitched with a smile, and he took another long pull straight from the bottle. "From your lips to my pocket. At six months, I bet on her for an indefinite stay."

He studied Fenton sourly. "Gambling is going to be your undoing."

"A single man must be allowed some vices." Fenton walked away, retreating to a sheltered spot where he could keep watch on everyone. Nicolas had several other servants scattered about the lake's edge, which is where the most likely danger would always be found.

Nicolas cast an eye over everyone and then turned to Mrs. Thorpe, who was still seated, skates on, eying the ice warily. "Are you truly nervous?"

"Only a little." She stood, appearing resolved to make an attempt. "I was taking a moment to pray that I do not fall. I don't miss the bruises I used to get or the embarrassment I caused myself as a girl."

He took her arm. "I told you I would never let you fall."

Together they staggered to the edge of the ice in their skates. Nicolas went first, skating a few steps before he turned to watch Mrs. Thorpe. She let out a breath and then stepped, smoothly gliding onto the ice as naturally as he did.

"See," he cheered. "You've forgotten nothing."

Gillian took off, revealing her skill was a fact, leaving Nicolas laughing in her wake. He caught up to her before she'd gone too far and together they glided in lazy swirls around the other skaters. He kept watch over her. Her cheeks were flushed a pretty pink and her hair fluttered beneath her bonnet. Her smile was radiant, and his heart filled suddenly with yearning. He wanted to touch her, hold her, very badly, right now, no matter the impropriety. "Ready?"

"For what?"

He smiled warmly. "Let's dance."

"Dance? Here?"

Nicolas nodded.

"I thought Jessica was joking about that."

"Oh, no," he promised. "I've tried to teach Jessica, to no avail, and have been searching for the right partner for years."

He held out his hand, and after a moment, Gillian caught it. Nicolas drew her to face him, and glided with her backward. "It is just like dancing on a ballroom floor. You follow my lead, and I do the hard work of pushing you about."

He put his hand firmly on her hip, and held her other arm straight out, clasping her gloved fingers tightly as if they were waltzing. He looked down into her face and was struck by the urge to kiss her. Now. He cleared his throat instead. "We'll start like this, but I'm sure to change our positions, so be prepared for anything."

"All right."

Nicolas pushed forward, driving Gillian ahead of him, weaving carefully around other skaters until he was sure they were a good match for this. He spun Gillian out and then tucked his body close behind hers. His hand returned to her waist, the other holding her hand. "You're very good," he murmured.

"So are you." She glanced over her shoulder to see his face. "When was the last time you tried this with another woman."

"Two years ago. Last year, I had to be content with skating all alone." ·

She pulled a face. "Oh, how you must have suffered, your grace."

He pulled her tighter against him, lifted her and pivoted, so they both were now skating backward together. Gillian gave a little shriek.

He glanced over his shoulder as he turned them in a wide arc and into clear ice before he lowered her slowly until she was skating again. "Shall we try that again?"

Gillian nodded, but the second attempt was a little more awkward than the first because she tensed in anticipation.

"You didn't trust me," he whispered as they stumbled, almost falling together. They got their skates under them and parted. "You have to trust that I know what I'm doing."

"I do trust you." Gillian brought her hand to her chest and stopped. "But I think it was better not to know what was coming," she said then laughed. "That was wonderful, your grace."

"It was." He stopped inches away from a collision with her. "That is two wonderful things we do well together, Gillian."

Gillian blushed and again laughed merrily. "I suppose it is."

Nicolas caught her elbow and Gillian pressed her hand to his chest. "Can we keep doing them together?"

Gillian gasped, eyes warming on his. "I'd like that."

"Wonderful, because I have to say I have never suffered an erection while skating before. Having you in my arms again is doing crazy things to my senses."

"Mine too," she confessed.

"I want to kiss you." Nicolas glanced past her head and saw four skaters headed their way at a fast clip. "Unfortunately, the pleasure will have to wait until we are truly alone again."

Gillian turned out of his arms to view the approaching group. "They're not skating well."

"No, they are not. Fledging chickens have more grace. I have no fears for Jessica or Whitfield, but I wonder if the other two are skilled at stopping."

"They're going a bit too fast if they are not." Gillian skated backward as the group showed no sign of slowing down.

Nicolas glanced at her suddenly as the ice gave a great crack beneath her feet.

"Gillian!" he cried, just before she dropped into the icy water with a shriek of utter terror that made his blood run cold.

Chapter Eight

———•———

"Oh!" Gillian cried out. She gasped at the vast cold burning the lower half of her body but she took stock of her situation quickly. She stood in hip-deep icy water of the lake, her skirts floating inelegantly atop the water, her legs already trembling and her feet still strapped to her skates. It could have been so much worse. She could have plunged straight down to her death rather than where she seemed to be—stuck and about to freeze.

"Don't move," Nicolas demanded from three feet away, his expression terrified.

Gillian held out a hand to warn him back as she tested her footing. Her position seemed solid enough for the moment.

"Do not take one step. You're only on the outcrop."

Looking about her again, she suddenly remembered there had been a very small finger of land jutting far out into the lake when she'd first arrived at the estate in the spring. Subsequent rains and the winter must have lifted the height of the water and then covered it completely in ice as winter progressed.

She glanced at the ice Nicolas stood on as he moved nearer. "Don't you come any closer or you'll fall through too," she warned him, determined to keep him safe.

The group of skaters she'd tried to avoid had already stopped, far enough away that they should not be in any danger themselves, or to Nicolas. "Move back all of you, now."

Nicolas and the others grudgingly skated back a yard. "I won't leave you," he promised her.

"You must," she pleaded as her teeth began to chatter. She glanced at the shore and saw servants gathering. "I'm safe for now. Only very cold. Get off the ice. Please don't worry for me. Help is already coming. See?"

Gillian turned her head farther toward the shoreline. There was a large body of ice between her and landfall and she wasn't sure how to get herself out of the water, but she had faith that she'd be rescued soon. Lord Stapleton's men were approaching the edge of the ice, two carrying ice picks.

"We're coming, Mrs. Thorpe," the steward called. "Just stay where you are."

Gillian couldn't be entirely still. She was afraid her body would grow numb, so she flexed her legs to keep her circulation going. The little waves she stirred sent splashes of cold higher up her body, and she had to hold her hand to her stomach to survive the discomfort.

Nicolas was on land when she looked around next and surrounded by a crowd. "That's it. Stay calm," he called.

Gillian shivered as her gown slowly became saturated with water and sank down around her legs and tangled about them. The weight of them would pull her under if she slipped and lost her footing. Stapleton's men started to chip at the ice in earnest, wading out to her very slowly.

She was shaking violently when one strong arm wrapped around her waist and towed her through the icy slush. Jessica stood restrained in her father's arms, a blanket clutched to her chest, her expression terrified.

"I'm fine," Gillian promised the girl as, at last, she stepped onto solid ground.

"You're not fine. You're turning blue," Stapleton complained as she reached them.

Stapleton wrapped her upper body in the blanket while his daughter fell to her knees to squeeze water from her skirts. Stapleton pulled her into his arms, into the very coat he wore so well too. The heat of his body was almost painful. She tried to push him away, but she was shaking too badly to affect him.

The steward pushed a bottle of spirits under her nose and made her drink a bitter mouthful. Gillian struggled with the first, but since it would help her ward off the chill, she swallowed a second mouthful. A second blanket was wrapped tightly around her lower portions and she was forced to walk a few painful steps with Stapleton's aid after her skates were removed.

"Can you feel your feet?" he asked when she stumbled.

"Yes, but they are very painful."

"Better get her into a warm bed as soon as you can, your grace," Fenton advised. He pushed his bottle against her lips once more and, already feeling the affects, Gillian took a third mouthful. "Get her into bed and keep an eye on her toes."

"I intend to." Stapleton swept her up into his arms suddenly and started back toward home without another word to anyone.

Jessica and Whitfield hurried ahead with the promise to warn the household.

Alone with Nicolas, Gillian shivered against his chest violently. "I didn't do that just to have you hold me."

"You don't know how lucky you are." His jaw tightened, and then he hugged her so tight she could feel his fingers digging into her thigh. "Another yard in my direction and you would have been in water well over your head. You scared me half to death, woman."

"Sorry." Gillian turned her face into his chest to warm her skin. Miserable and freezing, she closed her eyes and concentrated on breathing and the pain of her limbs as his steps jarred her body. She'd never felt so cold in her entire life. "I promise not to do that again."

"It wasn't your fault," Nicolas said as he brushed his lips against her brow. "It was mine for not being more observant."

"Shh," she whispered. "It was an accident."

Nicolas fell silent, holding her closer, and he hurried toward warmth. She didn't lift her head again until they were deep inside the house and heard Jessica issuing orders to everyone. Nicolas carried her all the way into her bedchamber.

"We must get her out of those wet things," Jessica suggested, stripping away the wet blankets and her outerwear as Nicolas slowly lowered her to her feet.

Gillian hobbled a few steps and grabbed a bedpost as she started to shake. "I think that's a fine idea."

"I'll build up the fire while you change," Nicolas promised.

Too numb to protest she could look after herself, or that the servants could, Gillian allowed her gown to be removed. But she was acutely aware that Nicolas was still in the room, working at the fire with his back turned for modesty's sake. Maids rushed into the room carrying all manner of things. She was too cold to care about such trivial details as propriety or the likely gossip they would spread later though the house.

When she was bundled in a fresh nightgown and the only robe she owned, she was helped into her bed, warmed by bricks placed about her feet and smothered in blankets.

Gillian bit back her whimpers as circulation returned to her extremities, feeling rather foolish. She should have been paying more attention to the ice and she'd ruined the duke's day. She huddled in a ball beneath the blankets as gentle hands pressed to her brow and asked her the same questions over and over. Her toes had never been so interesting before. Everyone who came into the room seemed to inquire about them.

"A physician has been sent for," Stapleton informed her.

Gillian glanced up and discovered the duke standing beside the bed, watching her with a grim expression.

"I'm fine," she promised him. "I don't need

a doctor."

"I'll be the judge of that." He turned slightly and she saw a line of servants behind him. "You may all return to your duties. Mrs. Thorpe will ring if she requires further assistance."

The housekeeper nodded and shooed everyone away. "Very well, your grace."

"I feared they'd never leave us alone." He leaned forward suddenly, kissed her brow and then dug beneath the blankets for her hand. He caressed her fingers in his warmer grip and then nodded. "Your feet next."

Gillian balked. She had no desire to come out from under the blankets yet. "They're fine. You should be getting back to your guests. It's not proper for you to remain."

"Do not argue with me," he warned. "Any familiarity between us will be forgiven under the circumstances."

He fell to his knees beside the bed, tunneled along under the blankets, and caught her foot in his warm hand. His fingers were gentle as he caressed her skin, and then he pinched the tip of each toe in turn. "Five toes?"

"I felt them all," she assured him.

"Now the other."

Gillian pushed her other foot toward him and suffered another intimate inspection that revealed her toes had not suffered any loss of sensation from the terrible cold. "You see? I'm perfectly fine."

Gillian attempted to sit up but he held her down by the shoulders. "You are to remain abed for the rest of today and tonight. Don't you dare move!"

"You're being silly, your grace." Gillian got out of bed. "Movement will be good for my circulation."

"Seeing you like that is havoc on mine," he promised before catching her against him. He held her in silence and then snatched a blanket off the bed to wrap her in. "What am I going to do with you?"

Gillian pushed him away. "I should see to Jessica," she began.

"She is in the next room, waiting her turn to fuss over you. I'm allowing her to retire from entertaining our guests for the rest of today and tonight." He frowned. "I've never seen her so terrified."

"As soon as I discovered I was on solid ground, I knew I would be all right." She tightened the blanket around her, well aware of her brush with death. "It just took a little too long to get out of the water without becoming chilled."

He drew close again. His arms were firm about her body, and so warm she sighed in pleasure. "Every moment seemed an agony for me until you were in my arms. Please, stay here tonight and rest. You don't have to remain in bed but it would please me very much if you had no chance to become chilled."

Nicolas' first wife had died of an infection in her lungs in this very house not long after Jessica was born, so Gillian knew where his fears for her health came from.

"All right, if you insist," she said, laying her hands upon his chest and patting him soothingly. "You may send Jessica in."

Nicolas dipped his head and kissed her cheek a few times. "Thank you."

"Try not to worry," Gillian murmured before stretching up to kiss his lips. It was brief and tender, with no bursts of passion hard on its heels.

Nicolas helped her back into bed, placing pillows behind her back, and pulled the blankets high up her chest so she would stay warm. His behavior was so sweet and tender. It had been a long time since she'd felt so cared for, and not even her husband had worried about her occasional illnesses the way Nicolas was doing now.

He took a few steps toward the door, and then hurried back. "I know you'll likely scold me, but I'll be back later tonight to see you," he whispered.

He stole another kiss, but he was gone before Gillian could insist that such a visit wasn't necessary or wise.

Jessica ducked into the room a moment later, scrambled across the bed and crushed Gillian in a fierce embrace. "I could have lost you."

"I'm fine, Jessica dear. I really am." Gillian's eyes filled with tears. She tried to hold them back but was unequal to the task. She might put on a brave face for everyone else, but Jessica felt too much like family. The daughter she'd never had and never could. She hugged the girl fiercely and sobbed against her shoulder. When the storm of weeping had passed, Jessica tucked them both into Gillian's bed without another word.

Chapter Nine

———•———

"Jessica was a bit put out with Whitfield teasing her today," Gillian whispered before she moaned as Nicolas nibbled her soft throat. She was trying her best to hold on to her decorum and keep to the usual topic of discussion but Nicolas thought she'd rather him continue making love to her than stop now.

"He always teases her," he whispered as he brushed across her nipples with the pads of his thumbs. He reveled in her excitement. Craved it more each time they came together. "What else?"

"She...ah." Her grip on the shelves tightened as he took the lobe of her left ear between his teeth and bit lightly.

Gillian shuddered.

Nicolas released her, chuckling quietly, and

drew back so she could finish her report.

Gillian turned slowly, using the shelving again to support herself. "You're a devil," she complained without malice.

Having heard the remark on a previous occasion, he grinned widely at hearing it again. Since Gillian's near drowning, and fast recovery, he'd indulged in a very wicked few days of mutual pleasure, and tonight he was intent on upping the stakes yet again. "I am with you."

With Gillian, he did things he'd only dreamed about before. He'd loved his wife but had never felt so hungry for more of a woman's kisses as he did with Gillian.

He was quite simply besotted by what they had shared so far. This felt right. Gillian indulged all his desires in private but in public he saw no outward sign that anything had changed between them. He was both pleased with that, and occasionally annoyed. "I am desirous of your company, conversation, and your body. Can I not have all three at once?"

The day she'd fallen through the ice had altered his plans for the future. Since that terrible day, Gillian's happiness and safety were always at the forefront of his mind. Having almost lost her so suddenly after finally finding her had brought home to him what was missing in his life.

He wanted a lover, a companion and a friend.

Gillian had become all of that for him and more.

She tossed her head from side to side. "So very hard to talk when you're kissing me."

He pressed his hips against hers firmly and her breath caught as she felt his erection against her sex. "That's why I was neglecting these sweet lips of yours, so I could hear you tell me of the hours we spent apart."

He'd long given up his self-delusion that these nightly meetings with Gillian had anything at all to do with his youngest daughter, if they ever had. If there was a problem with Jessica, he was confident Gillian would approach him at any time of the day. These nights had more to do with getting to know Gillian, and now he knew her very well indeed. He kissed her now as he'd longed to do all day when he'd been on his best behavior so as not to reveal their affair to all and sundry. The nights were theirs, just a short span of time he claimed to please them both until they were gasping and spent and had to part for propriety's sake.

Unfortunately, he couldn't be satisfied with their arrangement much longer. He longed to take her to his bed and spend the night worshipping her sweet body. To wake her, drowsy and warm from their lovemaking, and do it all again. And again, until dawn.

He had seen so little of her skin and was becoming desperate for a glimpse of the whole woman he bedded. But to do that required him to sneak into her bedchamber again or steal her away into his. Both situations could be disastrous for her reputation if they were caught together, and with his daughters and so many guests underfoot, it seemed impossible.

He couldn't bear for Gillian to suffer harmful gossip, so it seemed to him that he had but one recourse left. He swept Gillian into his arms, hugged her to his chest tightly a moment, and then carried her across the room to the desk.

But his mind was already fixed on the more serious and permanent solution of how to have Gillian where and when he liked.

The idea of keeping Gillian appealed tremendously. She had already become a fixed and natural part of his life. Jessica loved her in the place of a mother, and he, now they were alone so often and intimate, was growing more and more attached to her every day. He did not want to lose her when Jessica outgrew the need for a companion.

Nicolas needed Gillian for himself and himself alone.

He eased her down onto his desk and slowly

hitched her skirts to her knees, then widened her legs to stand between them. "Sweet Gillian, how you honor me again. You are so delightful."

She lowered her eyes demurely as she reached for the buttons on his trousers.

He stilled her fingers. "Don't be shy. Look at me."

Her eyes flashed open and lust swum in their depths. "I'm no longer shy around you. I can barely control my hands in my eagerness to touch."

He grinned, having had the same problem many times during the interminably long daylight hours. "I'm going to need many more sweet kisses and wicked touches tonight if I'm to survive another tomorrow."

"I see." She brushed her knuckles across his hard cock still confined in his trousers and grinned. "Like that?"

"I want everything and anything you grant me." He touched her face, noting it was as hot as her blush suggested. She had been a wife once, but had she even lusted after her husband like this? He'd been afraid to ask before tonight. Worried how he might fare in any comparison. Nicolas was certain he'd never experienced desire like this himself. He knew what that meant. He couldn't part with Gillian.

He would offer for her.

He should have considered marriage from the very first kiss they had shared.

Once married, he would never have to curb his desires again. He could not seem to stay away from her anyway, and so marriage seemed the natural path to take. This quiet desire of hers drew him in as if she shouted his name. He wanted to give her the right to do that without anyone disapproving.

He traced her jaw with his fingertip. "So lovely."

"So are you." Her face turned red. "Handsome, I mean."

"I'm pleased you think so." He kissed her brow softly, and then peppered kisses to her sweet lips. "I must admit you make me feel young again."

"I've never thought of you as old." Gillian toyed with the buttons on his waistcoat and then reached up to trace the bump on his nose. "At what age did you break this?"

"Seventeen." Seventeen and utterly controlled by lust in those days. He smiled. "I was found in a compromising position with my late wife before we married, and her brother took a swing at my head before he recognized who I was. After that, he was entirely affable and made sure the contracts for marriage were drawn up that very day."

"That's so young to get married," she said,

eyes wide.

A lifetime ago, it felt now. He'd changed, grown steadier and quite possibly a bit fustian at times. He was happy now though—happy to have discovered such peace and excitement with Gillian in his life. "My late wife was older and seduced me," he confessed, lest she think he was entirely to blame and a scoundrel.

Gillian spluttered. "Surely not."

"Well, this *is* the country," he grinned, and stole another kiss, enjoying telling her his secrets. "On balance, young men do tend to lose their virtue at a much younger age than women. All those haystacks and fresh air. I was already an earl and my wife wished to be a countess, so marriage suited us both. We had a good marriage, as you might have guessed from the number of children we had together. I've done my best to shield my daughters from similar situations that forced my marriage. I'd much rather Jessica not have the decision taken away from her because of curiosity."

A frown creased Gillian's brow. "She's not ready for marriage."

"I agree, but she must marry one day." He was pleased Gillian spoke from the heart about Jessica. She'd been dropping hints enough for the past month for even him to notice her concern was genuine, and not out of fear of losing her livelihood. It was important to him that Gillian speak her mind rather than always agreeing with him, but for the moment he was much more interested in uncovering Gillian's mysterious past. "How old were you when you married?"

"Twenty," she whispered and said no more.

"Did you love him very much?"

Gillian shook her head quickly, and Nicolas was relieved beyond words that it was so. He pressed a kiss to her cheek and teased her ear with his breath. If she'd never loved her late husband, it meant that all the space in her heart for love might be available to him in the future. "I'm so sorry."

"Thorpe wanted a young wife, and I thought marrying him was a sensible decision for a woman in my situation. I had only a small dowry and he was well enough to do that I thought I would never lack for the little comforts I might need in my life. Love had nothing to do with my decision to accept him."

Gillian had been widowed at four and twenty years. She'd mentioned the age once and he'd committed it to his memory. Four years after that she was a servant to his family. He suspected Wallace Thorpe hadn't left her much to live on to make her take such drastic measures. "And when he died. What did you think then?"

"I grew angry." She met his gaze, and the

look made his heart squeeze tight. "He left me with nothing to live on in his will, made no arrangements with his heir to ensure I had a roof over my head, which is why I took employment as a companion."

Nicolas made a vow. She would work no more. He would make her his duchess, a lady of leisure with all the comforts he could shower upon her. He held her tight a moment, making plans to see his London solicitor as soon as he returned to the capital. He would ensure the marriage contract provided her with everything she might need for a comfortable life upon his eventual death, too.

A brisk knock sounded on the door, scaring him out of his wits.

They'd never before been interrupted, and he stood stunned for a moment too long. The door rattled, but since it was locked, no one could come in.

"Father, the door is stuck again," Rebecca complained in a shockingly loud voice.

Thank goodness for the lock. His eldest daughter should have been abed at this late hour.

Gillian bounced out of his arms and hurried to straighten her clothes. She flew around the desk soundlessly, took her usual seat and folded her hands elegantly in her lap.

"Just a moment." Nicolas smoothed his hair,

his waistcoat.

He could see Gillian's chest rising and falling in panic, but she somehow kept her expression serene. If anyone glanced her way, they'd never suspect she'd been in his arms and aroused a few minutes ago. He admired her composure. For himself, he wasn't so calm or at all pleased by the interruption. At least when they married, he'd not have the worry of potential scandal over their heads anymore.

The door rattled again.

"Just a moment," he instructed again, casting a conspiratorial smile at Gillian. He caressed her cheek as he passed her chair, wishing he could just ignore the interruption and return to his conversation with Gillian. There was so much about her he wanted to know. "Let me see what I can do about it from this side," he called to his daughter.

He crossed the room, made a show of jiggling the handle in a bid to conceal the turning of the key. Since he'd used this trick before on his daughters and had never been caught out, he was certain she'd be deceived yet again.

The door sprung open when he finally turned the handle properly.

"You really need to have a servant attend to that door," Rebecca complained as she burst into his study uninvited.

"When this house party nonsense is done, I will," he promised.

Rebecca paused when she saw Gillian seated before the desk, a sour expression forming. Rebecca glanced between them, suspicion turning her eyes into hard slits. "I hadn't realized I was interrupting."

Gillian stood and curtsied to his daughter but said nothing.

Nicolas was well aware that Rebecca's distrust of pretty women stemmed from having discovered her own husband in bed with their housekeeper once before his death, so he stepped between them. He gestured Gillian back down into her chair.

"You *are* interrupting." Nicolas ignored Rebecca's shocked expression and returned to his side of the desk. "How can I help you?"

"I'd rather speak to you alone," she said.

"Can it not wait until morning?" he asked.

"No, Father."

He didn't want to send Gillian away, but suspected Rebecca wouldn't speak of whatever nonsense was on her mind until she was gone. The sooner they had this conversation, the sooner it would be over.

He might have to forgo the comfort of his lover for one night most likely too, but it couldn't be helped. He grabbed a book at random from his bookcase. "Very well. Mrs.

Thorpe, would you please peruse this volume and if you deem it suitable, please share it with my daughter when you can."

She stood quickly and stretched for the book. "Of course, your grace. Was there anything else?"

He dropped it lightly in her hand, wishing he could say more to ease any sting his dismissal might inflict. "Return it to this room when you're done," he said, then gestured her to the door gently, hating that he must keep up the act of master and servant a little longer.

As she moved away, Nicolas noted one of the buttons of her gown had come undone at the back. Most likely he'd done it himself when he'd been teasing her. Fearing his daughter's sharp eyes, he followed Gillian to the door, putting his body between his lover and his child.

"Goodnight, your grace. Mrs. Warner." Gillian departed and he breathed a sigh of quiet relief. That had been much too close for comfort.

He hadn't even turned around before Rebecca began. "Now, we need to discuss my sister. Jessica cannot continue rusticating in the countryside."

Nicolas sat behind his desk again and leaned back to observe his daughter. Since her husband's passing, this daughter had become the most frustrating and opinionated creature on the earth. "I suppose you have some plan for what I should do about that?"

"Yes. She needs to mingle with people of her own class. She needs to be in London as soon as possible. I propose taking her with me when I leave."

Nicolas skewered her with a sharp stare. "I will decide when and where Jessica goes, madam."

"She must be with other women." Rebecca leaned forward. "She has no idea how to command a room. I've warned you before that a companion cannot teach her everything she must know about how to conduct herself in society."

That would also be impossible to learn if Jessica was in Rebecca's shadow, too, but in his and Gillian's line of sight she might be happier doing so.

Going to London together was actually a very good idea. He did now have business to attend to with his solicitor if he was to be a husband again. Nicolas also had friends there he was keen for Gillian to become acquainted with. He could show Gillian about Town, spoil his daughter at the same time, and participate in Jessica's preparations for the coming season. There would be no battle over spending or choices that way. "I concede that some time in

London before the season begins might be beneficial."

His daughter sighed heavily. "After the party?"

"Yes, after the party, of course," he agreed. He would need a little time to woo his future wife though. They'd never spoken about marriage, or a future, only ever discussing the next time they could be alone together.

After the party, after he'd proposed to Gillian, he'd discuss the idea of a longer London excursion for all of them, and see how she felt about marrying by special license there. A month-long wait for the banns to be read would feel interminable, now he'd made up his mind to marry.

"And while Jessica is busy, you must give serious thought to the future of the family," Rebecca demanded.

He frowned at her remark. He already had a large enough supply of male heirs, three sons, four grandsons from two of them, to guarantee the succession. "Such as?"

"Finding a wife to look after the little things a little better around here," Rebecca said, gazing at him with pity in her eyes. "Stapleton needs a mistress again. I know you loved mother, but even she would say it is long past time for you to select her replacement."

Nicolas schooled his features as a grin tried

to break free. He was well ahead of Rebecca's plans for him. "I have already considered remarriage."

His daughter smiled. "So you will bend your attention to courting a lady this season?"

He didn't need the sort of lady Rebecca had in mind. Would he need to keep the news from his daughters until the last moment? Unfortunately, yes. This daughter would definitely disapprove of him marrying a lady who'd been working as a companion. Gillian was perfect for him—lusty, lovely and lively. Traits he needed very much in his life on a permanent basis. All he had to do was convince her to say yes.

He nodded. He'd start an official courtship tomorrow and marry before the season began if Gillian agreed.

He was certain Gillian loved Jessica, and he hoped she might love him too. Given what they'd already shared in this room, and hers, he believed she must already feel a strong affection for him. How many times had they made love now? Seven or eight, and the night of her accident, they'd made love twice in the short hours they'd been together.

He was going to marry Gillian as soon as the Christmas nonsense was over. He could barely wait till they were alone again. Just the three of them rambling about Stapleton and in

London.

Having thought she'd won, Rebecca bid him good night and swept from the room smiling broadly, leaving Nicolas to plan his first ever courtship. He laughed softly at the novelty. He seemed to be going about this marriage business entirely backward, but how else could he have known his heart if he'd not taken a risk?

If not for that wretched mistletoe in his pocket, he'd never have come to know Gillian Thorpe.

He climbed the steps to his bedchamber, cast a longing glance toward Gillian's distant doorway, but moved on to spend the night imagining how delightfully he and Gillian would enjoy the long hours of their wedding night.

And the hundreds of nights that would come after, when they would share a bed and love each other all night long.

If she might one day love him the way he hoped.

Chapter Ten

"The duke has agreed and that is that," Mrs. Warner informed the gathered ladies with a huge smile, utterly delighted with the devastating news she was sharing.

Gillian's heart sank. She could hardly believe she'd misjudged Nicolas' intentions so very badly. He knew Jessica wasn't ready for marriage and still he would push her out of home to find a husband. "I cannot believe it."

"The duke does as he pleases," Mrs. Warner scowled her way, and then shrugged. "Men tire so easily of women's concerns unless it suits their purpose, and Stapleton is no different."

"Why isn't he telling me this himself?" Jessica protested.

Mrs. Warner smiled at her sister. "Be happy, Jessica. He is at last being sensible. He has indulged you, but he must live his own life. He has admitted he longs for companionship and will marry. He will undoubtedly choose a young lady of quality with an impeccable pedigree this season. Knowing my father as well as I do, he will already have picked her out and is just waiting for the right moment to make the announcement. Which will be soon, of course."

"Who?" Jessica clung to Gillian's hand tightly. "Papa wouldn't marry without telling me first."

Mrs. Warner glanced about the assembled ladies with a smug expression. Her friends straightened, smiling widely at everyone as if they knew more than they could say. "I suspect he's already begun his courtship. It is just a matter of time before there is a wedding announcement in the London papers. St. George's, of course. I expect that is why he is sending you to me."

Gillian patted Jessica's hand. It couldn't be true. Jessica would never be so ruthlessly discarded by her doting father. Mrs. Warner must have misunderstood him about Jessica's future.

"But this is excellent news for us too," Mrs. Hawthorne exclaimed. "Mrs. Thorpe will be free to come to work for me now, and guide my dear Natalia toward her own happy marriage."

Mrs. Hawthorne smiled broadly at Gillian as if her prayers had been answered. Gillian just stared at her. Surely she didn't actually believe Mrs. Warner about this. And surely the Hawthorne's could not afford to employ another servant, let alone the wages of a companion, after all she'd heard of their situation. "Will I?"

Mrs. Hawthorne leaned forward, eyes pleading. "Oh, do say you'll come work with my daughters, Mrs. Thorpe. Everything will work out perfectly for all of us if you do."

Gillian willed Jessica to be silent for a moment and think of who was sharing such bad news and why. Mrs. Warner had always tried to manage Jessica, like a doll or plaything. They may be sisters but the woman rarely listened to opinions that differed. "I have a position here."

"Which will not continue when Jessica comes to live with me," Mrs. Warner informed her briskly. "You cannot remain where you are not needed. Jessica will have *my* staff to take care of her. *My* guidance. No more gallivanting around this estate in a condition no properly bred young lady should be in. No more inappropriate conversations with unacceptable men. No more talk of fungus at the dinner table. It is high time I took over the girl's education. She's nearly ruined as it is."

Mrs. Hawthorne gaped at Mrs. Warner, and as a worried frown filled her face, Gillian's heart sank. Mrs. Hawthorne must regret her impulsive offer of employment now after that outpouring of spite. If Mrs. Warner spoke the truth of Nicolas' plans, she would do her best to make Gillian unemployable too, just because Gillian had always spoken up when she disagreed over Jessica's upbringing. "Her father has voiced no objections to my instruction."

"What father truly knows what is best for an impressionable young woman in this day and age, I ask you?" Mrs. Warner shrugged and the gesture infuriated Gillian. "How can the girl make a suitable match if she's left to rusticate here?"

"That is true," Mrs. Hawthorne said softly, her gaze downcast. *Worried.* The Hawthornes could not afford the expense of a London season for their daughter, and everyone knew they depended on Natalia to make an excellent match.

Gillian caught Mrs. Hawthorne's eye. "Natalia is pretty and accomplished enough to have her pick of any number of gentlemen when she comes out this spring."

The girl was perhaps a bit too forthright at times, but was sure to choose wisely if given the right guidance. All she needed was to show a little more restraint when she met a new gentleman and she'd make a good match.

Mrs. Hawthorne beamed. "Thank you. I have such hopes for her and her younger sisters."

If Nicolas did dismiss her earlier than she'd expected, and she took up the offered position with the Hawthorne's, Gillian could very well be companion to the Hawthornes' brood for years to come. She might never have money to spare again, the wages she was accustomed to receiving might have to be drastically cut, and she might have to hoard the money she'd saved for her old age, but remaining here would mean she might still be able to see Jessica from time to time.

Gillian forced a smile, but had the time to end her affair with Lord Stapleton arrived? She could not begrudge him the chance to be happy with another woman if he was done with her. He'd made her no promises. "I'd be very pleased to help you with your daughters, Mrs. Hawthorne, *if* Lord Stapleton does indeed mean to release me from his employment."

"He can have no interest in stopping you from going where you are wanted," Mrs. Warner exclaimed, dismissing her cruelly as if she were less than nothing to anyone.

Smarting inside, seething in impotence, Gillian forced herself to hide any true emotion and inclined her head gracefully.

Jessica shrank away from her. "My father would never send me away. He loves me."

"Indeed he does," Gillian promised.

Mrs. Warner looked upon Jessica with a calculated gleam in her eye. "You leave with me, dear sister. Everything is arranged, so there is no point arguing about it. I have already written to engage a proper music master to begin your instructions as soon as we return home. There will be fittings and dancing instruction and all the little things a companion can hardly know about for you to learn. We shall start over from scratch and truly make something of you."

Jessica burst to her feet. "No! This is my home. I'm not going anywhere with you!"

Mrs. Warner sighed. "Young lady, properly raised young women do not yell. Ever. Mother would be so disappointed in you."

Jessica gasped and fled the room.

Mrs. Warner had said the one thing that was unforgivable. Mentioning the mother Jessica had never known but longed for was cruel. Gillian stood to follow. "Excuse me."

"No, leave her be," Mrs. Warner said before turning to Mrs. Hawthorne. "This is exactly why she should have been in my care all along."

Gillian shook her head stubbornly. "I am still the Duke of Stapleton's employee, and he would not want his daughter neglected when she is upset. You have no idea how badly you just hurt her feelings by mentioning her mother in such a way. Excuse me, Mrs. Hawthorne, Miss Hawthorne. Ladies. I must see to my duties."

She hurried after her Jessica, certain Mrs. Hawthorne's offer of employment would come to nothing now. Which would leave her with exactly no place to go at short notice. She had money enough for the inn and mail coach to a place of new employment. She'd decide her direction later, but for the moment her first priority was making sure Jessica calmed down before she did anything she'd regret later.

When distraught, the girl usually went to one of two places—to her room, or out to the orangery. Since her bedchamber was empty, Gillian headed outside after procuring her heaviest cloak to keep her warm. Snow had been falling since daybreak and it was not difficult to detect footsteps headed in the direction of the distant building. She paused as she noticed a second, larger and deeper pair besides Jessica's coming from the direction of the house too. Had Lord Stapleton followed his daughter from the house?

He was undoubtedly the best suited to reassuring the girl about this change of plans, but it would still be wise to see if she were needed anyway.

She slipped into the orangery and quickly shut the door to keep in the heat. Stapleton's gardens boasted many such outbuildings. Forcing houses, walled gardens and more. There were so many places to explore with Jessica that appealed to the young girl's curiosity and love of nature, while not technically being in the out of doors.

She looked to the end of the long room—and froze.

Jessica stood in the arms of a man who was most definitely not her father, and was crying piteously against the fellow's dark cloak. His face was lowered to Jessica's head, and as Gillian watched, he kissed her hair, her brow. He gently cupped the back of the girl's head and seemed to be making love to her.

And Jessica was doing absolutely nothing to stop him.

Gillian loudly cleared her throat and the gentleman sprang back as if burned.

Gillian scowled. "Mr. Whitfield?"

He swallowed and glanced about him with a decidedly guilty expression. "Mrs. Thorpe. It's not what you think."

Gillian had seen those gentle kisses, and his bright blush confirmed her suspicions about his not-so-harmless interest in Jessica. She hurried forward and pulled the witless girl to her side. "Are you all right?"

Jessica nodded, hugged herself, and began sobbing anew.

"Oh Jess, darling. Do not cry." Gillian took the girl into her arms and stared at Mr. Whitfield. "If you orchestrated this meeting for any untoward purpose I shall throw a pot at you, and then inform Lord Stapleton you cannot be trusted with his daughter."

"No!" The man paled. "I didn't follow her. I was already here, admiring Stapleton's new raised flowerbeds. I swear, I turned around and she threw herself into my arms."

The man appeared sincere, but those kisses meant something else entirely. "I see."

He rubbed the back of his neck. "She *is* crying."

Gillian found a handkerchief she kept in the pocket of her coat and dabbed at the girl's damp cheeks. "It will be all right," she whispered.

"No, it won't," Jessica wailed. "It's going to be simply horrible."

"May I ask what is wrong?" Whitfield asked.

"I lost my mother...now I am to lose my companion," Jessica wailed. "I am to move to London and live with Mrs. Warner. I hate London. I hate Papa for sending me away!"

"You don't hate him," Gillian disagreed.

Mr. Whitfield appeared confused. "I thought you were looking forward to being out."

"I shouldn't have to leave my home for that to happen."

"No, of course not." The man glanced Gillian's way, frowning. "Why send her away?"

"I've no idea." Gillian sighed. She could not shake the embarrassment that she had failed the girl and not detected Stapleton's displeasure with her teaching methods. Everyone had said the girl had mellowed since Gillian's arrival, but apparently not enough to make her presentable to society without her sister's intervention and influence. "It has apparently been decided that Jessica should spend some time with Mrs. Warner's circle of friends before the season begins."

"I am to be polished and made into a proper lady." Jessica scowled again. "Mrs. Warner also says Papa is about to marry, too, which I cannot believe is true."

He stared at them both. "Stapleton would tell you first if he had decided to remarry," Whitfield promised.

Jessica sniffed. "I hope so."

"I cannot imagine what would make him send you off to live with Mrs. Warner. He would not change a thing about you, Jessica. You are entirely without equal."

Despite her upset, Jessica began to chuckle. "That is by far your most outrageous bit of flattery to date, Whitfield. I will miss our silliness and long walks."

"So will I." He pressed his lips together tightly, and then bowed. "Since your companion is on hand to offer you support, I should take my leave. Perhaps we might talk again before you go."

"I'd like that," Jessica promised. "Who knows when I might have leave to be myself again, as I am when I am with you. We have yet to discuss the growing of mushrooms."

He smiled. "As always, the discussion of fungus at dinner enlivens my evenings immensely. Mrs. Thorpe, it will be a tragedy for the district if you leave Stapleton. You have made quite an impression on everyone here."

"I might not go far in the end," she mused. "Mrs. Hawthorne has just offered me a similar position to the one I have now."

"That was very swiftly done," Whitfield suggested, frowning. "I trust it is what you want."

What she wanted was to stay until Jessica found a man worthy of her affection. She forced a smile. "Serendipity. A fortunate accident of timing, I'm sure."

Whitfield did not appear convinced. But he nodded and took his leave.

Gillian waited a moment, and then held Jessica firmly by her shoulders. "What happened between you and Whitfield?"

The girl shrugged. "I mistook him for father, but by the time I noticed, I'd already been crying on his coat several minutes. He bore it well."

Gillian was relieved. For a moment there, she had wondered if Whitfield had followed Jessica for an assignation. Jessica, of course, would never suspect his motives might have been less than pure, but Gillian saw his interest very plainly.

"Very well." She tipped Jessica's chin up. "May I offer you a piece of advice?"

"Of course." Jessica caught her hand tightly. "I'd much rather hear yours than my sister's any day."

"Do not let anyone know Whitfield held you in his arms today, especially not Mrs. Warner."

"Well, I do not confide in her ordinarily, but can I tell my father how kind he was?"

Gillian caressed the girl's cheek. Had Gillian ever been so clueless when it came to the intentions of men? "Do you want to be married to Whitfield?"

The girl appeared horrified. "Marry Giddy?"

"He is considered by many—not Mrs. Warner, of course—to be a very eligible bachelor." When the girl continued to stare, Gillian continued. "He is handsome, kind and wealthy enough to please many a parent. He could afford a family if he chose a wife. It is easy to see he likes you very much, and you like him too. He is also your papa's friend, and I cannot think of a reason the duke would deny the match."

The girl tipped her head to the side. "I like to talk to him. Giddy makes me laugh like no one can."

"If that is the whole of your interest in him, then please make sure never to be alone with him again. People could misunderstand your relationship."

Jessica's eyes filled with tears. "How will I survive without you in London? You're my best friend in the whole world."

Gillian rubbed Jessica's arm. "You will thrive in London whether I am there or not. I could never be your companion forever."

"Father is not being fair."

"Don't say that," she said quickly to head off a tantrum. "His grace takes more interest in your future than any father I've ever known. Please don't be difficult about this if it is true. For my sake, if nothing else."

Jessica's bottom lip trembled. "Well, it's not best for you to live with Miss Hawthorne and her sisters. They're like wild animals. Natalia is still making eyes at Papa. Thank you for helping him avoid her this past week."

"I haven't helped him do any such thing, and he's much too assured to need any assistance from a paid companion. He will choose well, never fear." He'd never want Gillian for more. She was only a diversion from loneliness. Her heart pinched with unbearable pain still but she'd always known that to hope was to reach too high. "Have faith that your father knows what he's doing is best for you."

"I'll never forget you." Jessica embraced her, squeezing tightly. "Will you write to me?"

"Of course." Gillian kissed the girl's hair. In all the time she'd lived at the estate, she'd become very fond of the girl, tantrums and all. If Gillian ever married again and had a daughter, she'd name the child Jessica in remembrance of these happy months at Stapleton. "Nothing would please me more. I will always think of you and hope you are happy wherever you may find yourself."

Chapter Eleven

———————•———————

One more day until the guests were due to depart. The longer it took to speak the words that filled his heart, the more nervous about the outcome Nicolas found himself. He'd even welcome the fisticuffs that had marked the beginning of his first engagement if it assured him of a favorable outcome.

Nicolas paused beside Gillian. "You are quiet tonight."

Gillian startled but then smiled. "Am I?"

"Jessica is subdued too." He observed his daughter carefully, looking for a cause of distress, and saw nothing obvious. She was seated beside Whitfield on the chaise across the room and appeared to be deep in conversation with him, most likely about their mutual interest in plants and nature. He was pleased his friend had returned to the gathering and made an effort to engage his youngest daughter in conversation. Whitfield could be depended upon.

On the whole though, he'd become disappointed with this gathering. Nothing had really changed. Rebecca had promised that Jessica would have a chance to meet people. He'd thought she'd meant a younger-aged set. The only good to come of this Christmas was that he'd fallen hard for Gillian Thorpe, and he couldn't wait to tell her. "Have you had a difficult day with her?"

"No, we had a very pleasant day. She took to her lessons eagerly this morning and then enjoyed luncheon with her sister. Later we spent some time in one of the forcing houses." She swallowed. "How was yours?"

"Busy. I tell you truly that I cannot wait until everyone is out of my hair."

Her chin lifted and she smiled at something across the room. "I'm very sure you will be happy to have your peace restored."

"I am sorry about last night," he whispered, just as Jessica gestured to Gillian to come to her. "My daughter and I had a chat last night and the plans for Jessica's coming season have been improved somewhat."

Gillian's heart sank. Mrs. Warner had been correct after all.

"That is wonderful." Gillian glanced at him quickly. "Please excuse me, your grace. Jessica needs me."

When she walked away, Nicolas considered following her, taking her into his arms, and proving he needed her, too. But the room was full of people who would not take kindly to watching him kiss the woman he loved witless. They would not understand how difficult he was finding the waiting. It seemed nearly impossible to steal just enough time to string more than a handful of sentences together today, and he'd had so much more to say and no opportunity to do so.

Jessica bounced to her feet and caught Gillian's hands. They moved aside toward a window, whispering furiously together. Jessica tugged her toward the hall, but Gillian resisted. She planted her feet as if she were an immovable object.

Nicolas hid a smile. He could sympathize with his daughter's desire to leave all too well, and silently applauded Gillian's refusal to give in to the girl. He exhaled slowly.

Patience was not his strong suit. He and Jessica had that in common. He wished he had a way to get everyone to leave right now without them knowing why.

Whitfield stood, came across the room, and shook his head. "Poorly done."

"What?"

"That." He gestured toward Jessica and Gillian, who now seemed to be arguing.

Jessica and Gillian glanced his way at the same moment and both looked away quickly. Had that been tears in Gillian's eyes?

Concerned, Nicolas hurried toward her. "What is the matter?"

"Nothing of consequence, your grace," Jessica murmured, shocking him to his boots. His youngest daughter had never once addressed him by his title in her entire life.

Whitfield appeared beside Jessica, and they exchanged a long look. She nodded eventually, but then smiled brightly at Nicolas. "Was there something on your mind?"

Gillian appeared too calm. Almost serene.

"I, ah," he began, but Nicolas was utterly baffled. He caught Gillian's eye quickly. "Mrs. Thorpe, might I have a word in private?"

Jessica tightened her grip on Gillian's hand, eyes pleading. "She has a headache."

He turned on Gillian. "Is that true?"

"Only a slight one, your grace."

"Well, this will only take a moment, and then you must go upstairs to rest immediately," he decided. There was no need for her to stay if she was unwell.

"I will rest soon enough," Gillian promised, and then kissed Jessica's cheek before she was finally released. "Please excuse me, Mr. Whitfield."

"Of course," Whitfield promised.

"This way." Nicolas led her toward the entrance hall and paused there, in sight of everyone but still private enough that their conversation would not carry. "I've been trying to speak with you alone all day."

Gillian shivered and her eyes rose to his. "Jessica needed me. You know how she can be."

"I need you too," he whispered. The look she gave him was far more serious than in recent days. Did she feel the change coming? She must see how very good they were together. Was she waiting for him to go down on bended knee before everyone now? He would not do that. He intended a very private proposal, followed by a great many kisses to celebrate when she agreed. "Come to my room tonight after dinner. There's something we need to discuss."

Her eyes widened. "What if someone were to see me?"

"No one will," he promised. He had intended to ask for her hand in marriage as soon as his guests departed, but he couldn't wait for tomorrow. It would not be the best beginning for their marriage to rush, but if they were found out, he was comforted by the fact that any scandal would be short lived. A month at most of unpleasantness and then happiness forever. "Please, Gillian. Find a way to come to me. I will wait all night if need be."

Her chest rose and fell quickly, exposing her anxiety. She liked the idea but not the risk, and he could understand her hesitation. She did not know what was in his heart yet. She had to take it on faith that all would be well.

"I'll try," she whispered.

She slipped back into the drawing room instead of retiring, smiled at Jessica, and the pair remained inseparable all night, only parting long enough to take dinner at opposite ends of his dining table—mother and daughter already.

Chapter Twelve

———•———

Gillian slipped into Nicolas' bedchamber as all the clocks in the house stuck eleven. The hour was late, but this might be the last and only night she could be with him again.

The thought of leaving the duke had become unbearable as the day progressed.

She almost had the door closed when she spotted him asleep in a chair by the window. She drank in her fill of his looks, the open throat of his shirt, and when her heart clenched, she realized she shouldn't have come after all. She took a step back so as not to wake him.

Unfortunately, a board creaked beneath her foot and he woke immediately, and then smiled when he saw her. "Finally."

"I apologize." Gillian glanced around his

large chamber. She'd have tonight, one last memory of him to last her a lifetime. His huge bed, his slightly rumpled state. His long bare feet carrying him across the room toward her.

"The pleasure of having you in my arms is always worth the wait." He scooped her up and twirled her around. "I'm so glad to see you. There are so many things I need to say to you tonight."

Gillian didn't want to talk. She already knew the worst of it. Hearing him explain that she must leave would only make her cry. She brought her fingers to his mouth to stop his words, and then she replaced her fingers with her lips as he slid her down his body.

There was nothing more to say than this.

She was a fool who'd lost her heart.

Nicolas kissed her back hungrily and carried her toward his bed, seemingly pleased with her impatience. Once on her feet again, he held her so tightly that she was afraid this was his goodbye too. Gillian hated partings, especially the inadequate words spoken that failed to soothe. So, she undid the buttons on her gown instead.

Even though her hands were shaking, she managed four before he aided her. "You're right, we can talk in the morning."

In the morning, she'd slip away and do her best to avoid him just to spare herself the pain of being dismissed.

When her gown was pushed down to the floor, and her corset and shift removed, Nicolas pulled his shirt over his head.

She gaped at his perfection, his obvious strength, the sleek lines of his body made her mouth water. He was broad across the chest but wiry muscles graced his shoulders and arms. His stomach was flat and his hips, the only real glimpse of his skin she'd had before, were snuggly contained in a pair of black silk breaches.

"Do I please you?"

Gillian swallowed the lump in her throat. She bowed her head, resting her brow against his hot skin while she grappled with her chaotic emotions. Gillian ran her hands up and down his sides, marveling in the texture of his skin and becoming aroused by his warmth. "Yes."

"There's nothing to be ashamed about in wanting to be with me."

"I am not ashamed." She was heartbroken. She cared about him. She loved him and Jessica so much. They'd become her family.

She forced the hurt back and looked up into his face. She put her hand behind his head and pulled him down for a deep kiss before he saw too much in her expression to begin asking questions about.

All he wanted was her passion, and he'd

have it all for this one last time. Tonight, she would know everything about his body and carry the memory of him forever in her heart.

She caressed the bulge in his trousers each time she drew back between kisses. "I need you."

Nicolas swept her onto his huge bed and climbed up next to her. He stretched at her side and brushed against her bare skin, making her passions rise in a way her husband never had. She loved him. She loved everything about this wonderful, horrible man.

Gillian curled her arms around his shoulders and buried her face against his skin so he could not see the depths of her pain.

Thankfully, he mistook her urgency for passion and slid down the bed. He was more than ready to make love to her. He buried his face between her legs, impatient and demanding that she be aroused by him, satisfied by his skilled lovemaking.

And she would be. Despite the future they wouldn't share, she craved his touch still.

She touched his head as he kissed her sex, and then lost herself in pleasure.

It did not take long before he had her poised at the edge of a release and she came, crying out and then sobbed hard, knowing he'd never kiss her there ever again.

The duke rose above her, loosened his

breeches, and shoved them down until he was bare from top to bottom. Then before she could memorize the slight curve of his cock, he wrapped her in his arms and joined with her. They fit together like two peas in a pod.

Every time they had made love before, there had been some awkwardness to overcome—a chair arm, a hard desk, shelving to distract her from what they were doing. She'd never realized how deeply she'd given herself over to Nicolas until he was inside her, sharing his bed, his body wrapped around her without a stitch of clothing between them.

This was love, passion, utter surrender to her own desires. Gillian hugged him close, losing herself in him. She wound her legs around his hips at his urging, her arms tight around his neck as he brought her closer to another release by just being with her like this.

He growled suddenly into her neck and held her tight as he shuddered and moaned her name without warning.

Overwhelmed by the warmth of his seed spilling inside her body, she came, too, smothering her cry into his shoulder, holding back the admission that she loved him.

When they settled, Nicolas rolled onto his back panting, keeping Gillian tight against his side. "I've been wanting to do that for so long."

Gillian bit back a sob.

"We can't keep sneaking around," he informed her. "It's better this way, isn't it?"

Gillian nodded, miserable to her core. She wasn't young but did he not realize that he might have gotten a child on her tonight? She'd thought she'd known him, but all she knew of him was what he'd chosen to reveal. "It is."

She was left with no illusions about her place in his life. She huddled at his side, listening as his breathing evened out, and when she realized he was deeply asleep, Gillian crept from his bed, dressed in a hurry and fled to her room without looking back.

She didn't wait for morning. Gillian was packed and ready to leave long before the sun ever rose.

Chapter Thirteen

———•———

Nicolas looped Jessica's arm through his and led her out of doors. She was subdued today again, so he'd stolen her away for a private word. She'd always been sensitive to his moods, and he feared she must have felt his impatience that the party end. He would tell her his plans today, swear her to secrecy, and then he was going to enlist her help to capture the elusive Gillian Thorpe alone at last. "Are you warm enough?"

She peered at him from under the two scarves he'd wrapped around her neck to ward off the chill of the cold morning. "I am very warm, thank you."

"Good."

He led her out into the snow-covered gardens, trampling across the lawns rather than risking their necks on paths that might be slippery with ice. He cast a glance behind him occasionally, checking no one was foolish enough to follow. "Are you well?"

"Yes."

She did not sound it. She sounded utterly miserable. "Would you tell me if you were not happy?"

Jessica hesitated. "If I thought it would do any good."

Nicolas stopped and faced his daughter. She meant the world to him, but he wanted Gillian to share his life too. It was important that his daughter understand that loving Gillian, marrying again, didn't mean he loved her any less. He wanted to expand their family and increase their happiness. "It has been just the two of us rattling about this house for a good long while, hasn't it?"

Jessica's gaze turned flinty. "You're going to marry."

He grinned, pleased that she'd reached the same conclusion as he had recently. It was time. "I am. How do you feel about that?"

"I don't like the idea."

He took his daughter's hands in his. "I *want* to marry. I promise that nothing will ever change. You will always be important to me."

Jessica sobbed. "I don't want to talk about that."

He brought Jessica into his arms and held her tightly. "I know. But I must think and act with honor. Your sister has been haranguing me for years on the topic and until now, I felt no inclination to take a wife."

"Well, if you're so set on marrying, I demand a fair exchange and I get to keep Gillian as my companion."

"That's not possible, sweetheart." He bent to whisper in her ear, "Gillian cannot remain your companion if I make her your new mother."

Jessica pushed him back violently. "You want to marry my companion?" she almost shrieked.

He held out his hand to shush her and glanced about them. There was no one around, but Jessica's voice might travel far on a cold day. "With all my heart."

Jessica turned away, strode a few steps before returning. Her expression was incredulous. "Rebecca said you were going to dismiss Gillian and you would make me live with her in London. Is any of that true?"

He shook his head firmly, but was unsure what to make of Jessica's reaction to his decision. Was she happy that he was in love or angry with him for choosing Gillian? Gillian would probably know which it was, but he could hardly have asked her to join them before he actually asked for her hand.

"Your sister sometimes hears only what she wishes to hear. I spoke to her about going to London *with* you *and* Gillian, of course."

"That deceitful cow tried to trick us!" A look of wonder crossed his daughter's face. "You would marry Gillian and come to London for the season, too, just for me?"

"No. I've fallen in love with Gillian, so the right thing to do of course is to ask for her hand in marriage and be wed. I had hoped we might be married in London right after the party guests leave. Discreetly, mind you, so your sisters cannot make a fuss about any rush and all that. What do you say to the idea that we explore the sights and sounds of London together, as a family, before the season truly begins?"

"With Gillian as my mother?" Jessica suddenly drew back, fingers raised to her lips. "Oh, dear."

"What? Don't tell me you disapprove of my choice? Were you not just asking to keep Gillian as your companion? Her being your mama will be much better for all of us, I promise."

Jessica jumped up and down. "Yes, I approve of my new mother!" She hugged him tightly, which reassured him that he would not have problems in the future from that quarter.

But she drew back soon enough, still frowning. "Mrs. Hawthorne is not going to be happy."

He tightened the scarf to cover Jessica's pink nose and held out his arm. "Time to return indoors before you catch a chill. It might surprise you that I don't particularly worry about Mrs. Hawthorne's happiness in the grand scheme of things. It is none of her business whom I marry anyway. I want to spend the rest of my life with Gillian, and I will, if she will have me."

Jessica winced but fell into step. "Mrs. Hawthorne has been trying to steal Gillian away to her employ for months. The news that you would send her away while I went to live with Rebecca has caused Gillian no end of pain and suffering."

"I see. Well, as you see, Rebecca was wrong and no one is being sent away."

"Do you really not understand, Papa?" Jessica stopped him. "Mrs. Hawthorne has succeeded. Gillian accepted the new position yesterday. She's already packed to leave."

"That's impossible. Last night we—" He bit his tongue on the rest of that confession. Last night they hadn't actually talked about anything important. They'd made mad, passionate love in his bed. He'd lost himself in Gillian because he'd thought it clear that he wanted her desperately and forever.

He turned back to stare at the house. Had he not been understood? That would mean Gillian thought him…an utter scoundrel.

"She would have told me," he said, but deep down he thought maybe she would not have.

"Well, it is true that she believes you don't want her around anymore." Jessica tugged on his hand, dragging him toward the house. "You must tell her right now that she does not need to go anywhere!"

"I will." He quickened his steps, and they met Whitfield at the nearest door.

The man folded his arms across his chest, a question in his eyes as he blocked their path.

Nicolas winced. "Where is she?"

"Papa is getting married again, Giddy," Jessica told Whitfield with a wink. "Mrs. Thorpe will be my new mother. I'm so proud of you! Your plan worked beautifully."

"What plan?"

"To get you wed." Whitfield pursed his lips, and then laughed as he pulled several clumps of mistletoe from inside his coat. "I guess I can stop hanging these about the place, now that you've seen reason."

"See that you do." Nicolas scowled and snatched them up, glancing at his daughter with newfound suspicion. "Did you put mistletoe in my pockets because he told you to?"

"Of course." Jessica twisted on the spot, grinning. "Who else do you allow to get that close?"

"Gillian. I accused her the first time." He nodded, and then protested as Jessica gave him a hard shove. He stared at his good friend and daughter, not liking their collusion one bit. "Do I need to keep you two apart?"

"Oh, don't. Giddy is my dearest friend, aside from Gillian, who will be my mama, which is entirely different." She pushed him again. "Go!"

"You're almost too late," Whitfield warned as he stepped aside. "The Hawthorne's carriage is already outside, waiting to take her to visit them today. I gave the Hawthornes' coachman a coin to be slow about turning the carriage round, to give you time. Try the long gallery."

He thumped his friend's shoulder. "Keep an eye on Jessica, please.

"I always do," Whitfield assured him with a wide grin.

Chapter Fourteen

———•———

"My dear, you have done wonders with Jessica. I'm so glad I will be able to steal you from Stapleton," Mrs. Hawthorne exclaimed as they stood before the hearth in the long gallery together while waiting for the Hawthorne's coach. "I'm sure a month with you can whip my daughters into shape."

"Natalia's a lovely girl." Gillian craned her neck, hoping for a glimpse of her current charge, who was out walking with her father. She wanted one last hug before she left to visit her new situation. "I am looking forward to spending time with them."

"Now, before we go, I want to make sure you understand that I haven't paid any heed to Rebecca's remarks yesterday. I know Jessica has changed for the better since your arrival. And I also know Rebecca's temperament well. Jessica is much calmer now than she used to be, and my daughter has certainly benefited from the numerous invitations to visit since you came to live here. I'm sure our inclusion was thanks to your influence over the duke."

Gillian shook her head, heart pained. "I had little influence on the duke's decisions." He didn't listen to her. If he had, he wouldn't be forcing Jessica to live with Rebecca.

She wished she could escape this kind woman before she broke down and cried her eyes out.

Gillian turned away—but gasped as Nicolas skidded sideways into the chamber, struggling to keep his balance on the highly polished marble floor. He straightened when he saw her, tugged his coat and strode toward her purposefully. Gillian's heart began to beat hard against her ribs in time with his steps, until she thought she might faint.

Mrs. Hawthorne beamed. "What brings you here in such a hurry, Stapleton?"

"My companion."

"My companion now." Mrs. Hawthorne smiled at Gillian fondly. "What you do not want, I will gladly take off your hands, your grace."

"It was my eldest daughter who claimed I didn't want her." He sidestepped his neighbor and loomed over Gillian. "I *do* want you, Gillian. Very much."

Gillian froze. "Your grace?"

"My love," he whispered, bringing his fingers up to caress her burning cheeks. He bent further, until his lips hovered inches over hers. "Last night was the beginning for us, not the end. Don't go. I love you with all my heart."

He paused a moment while she processed that news, and then he crushed her mouth under his in a devastating kiss that left Gillian without any doubt of his sincerity.

They were not alone!

Mrs. Hawthorne swooned, stumbling back against the nearest wall to gape and gasp.

Gillian clutched Nicolas for support, giddy with shock and hope. He bound her tight against his chest and lifted her feet from the floor. "Never, ever, ever, ever believe any of my children know my plans before you do."

"But Jessica?"

He smiled. "Will go to London with us when the house party ends, if you agree to marry me by special license as soon as possible."

"I..."

"Don't tell me you don't love me, now that I've gone and ruined your chances of employment with Mrs. Hawthorne." He glanced at his neighbor. "Sorry about that. Perhaps you should sit down."

Mrs. Hawthorne was already against the wall and, at his suggestion, slid to the marble floor, oblivious that her gown had risen above her knees and revealed her shapely legs.

Nicolas turned his warm and wicked face to Gillian and kissed her quickly again. "You love me. I know you do."

Gillian studied his face. So many things about his behavior suddenly made sense. His determination to protect her reputation, his insatiable desire, and his behavior the last time they'd made love. He'd wanted to talk, but she'd distracted him with kisses and then hid from him ever since. Armed with self-doubt and Rebecca's false information, Gillian hadn't given him a chance to speak his mind or his heart.

She held his gaze and then brought her hand to his dear face. "Heaven help me, I do love you."

He winked. "Then without further ado…"

He set her down and sank to one knee, took her hand in his and smiled up at her. "Darling Gillian, would you make me the happiest of men by accepting me as your husband? I promise to devote my life to making you happy, and I assure you my first appointment when we arrive in London is to have my solicitor draft a marriage contract that will ensure you will never have to raise another man's child as your own again."

She beamed at him. "I was very happy standing in for Jessica's mother all these past months."

"Then say yes, and become her mother in truth." He rose. "Let me love you for all the days of my life. I cannot bear the thought of ever losing you."

Gillian sobbed and raised her hand to his face. She had never heard such a sweet sound as Nicolas pleading for her love and hand in marriage. "Yes, Nicolas. I would be so happy to marry you."

Epilogue

———•———

"Remember not to get too comfortable." Nicolas squeezed Gillian's fingers one last time, stepped from the traveling carriage, and then turned to help his wife out. He kissed her fingers before he let her go.

Gillian looked around, grinning from ear to ear. "I have missed this place," she told him.

"We all have," Jessica said dryly, falling into place beside Gillian and looking around the grounds with a critical eye. "It's good to be back where we belong."

"We *are* going back to London once I've dealt with the situation," he warned his daughter. This was only to be a brief respite from the delights and rigors of the London season.

Jessica sighed. "I wish we could just stay here forever instead."

"And leave your new friends to face the perils of the marriage mart alone?" Gillian chided. "You'd never desert them in their time of need. Besides, there is no one better at driving away unwanted suitors than you with your talk of fungus."

That brought a smile to Jessica's lips. "It was Giddy's idea to bore them to death," she confessed.

"Good old Whitfield," he murmured, and then smiled as his staff poured out the front doors to welcome them home.

"Welcome home, Lord Stapleton, Lady Stapleton, Lady Jessica," their butler exclaimed as he hurried down the front steps, his coat tails flapping in his haste to greet them.

"Hello, Brown." It was clear his staff were eager to greet the new Duchess of Stapleton because all eyes were on her now. When Gillian had left the estate, she'd still been a companion, with only four souls aware of Nicolas' intentions to marry her. They had wed in London, two weeks after their arrival in the capital—a small gathering where Nicolas had barely acknowledged anyone. None of his children, beside Jessica, had been informed or invited. He hadn't wanted to overwhelm Gillian since she had no family to invite then and his own children might have raised a fuss over him marrying a woman recently employed in his household.

He was so in love with Gillian and the possibilities of their life together, he had hardly paid attention to his second wedding service.

He was told he'd become quite rude, too.

Because of his distraction, Gillian had had to win over his closest friends in London on her own merit. She was warm to them, even laughed at their ribbing of him being leg shackled again. They'd hosted two intimate dinners for friends in London before their return. But he could tell Gillian was a little lonely for her own friends, her lost family too, which was why he'd brought them back home under the pretense of dealing with an emergency on the estate.

Nicolas beamed as Gillian exchanged a kind word with the butler and housekeeper, moving smoothly into her new role of duchess with aplomb. She had been popular with everyone at Stapleton, and it appeared nothing had changed with her elevation. He was so proud of her he could burst.

"Should you like to look over the day's menus soon, your grace?" the housekeeper asked Gillian.

"In perhaps an hour, in the morning room." She touched her head with a small laugh. "I'm afraid I'm still rocking from the carriage just a bit too much to concentrate."

"Me too," Jessica quipped, before she kissed

Gillian's and Nicolas' cheeks. "I want the peace of my room for the afternoon and the new book on propagation that Giddy sent me."

"Very good." The housekeeper stepped back with a smile while Gillian spoke to the remaining staff. They all seemed happy to see Gillian, happy about their marriage, and he was well pleased with her reception.

"Make it two hours, Mrs. Brown," he suggested with a grin, placing his hand on the small of Gillian's back and steering her indoors. Nicolas considered them newlyweds still, and he desperately wanted to be alone with his wife in the place they'd fallen in love.

He put his arm around her shoulders as they ascended to the first floor, and then he hugged her to his side tightly. "We'll be here only a few days, my love."

She glanced his way. "Will you tell me now what the emergency is?"

"We have visitors expected tomorrow," he told her.

"Visitors?" Her brow rose. "Why be so secretive about that?"

"Well, I wasn't sure they could come until a few days ago, and I didn't want to disappoint you if they refused to come when I wanted them to."

"Who are they?"

Nicolas took her hands in his. "Your younger brother and his wife are coming to visit you."

Her breath caught and her eyes widened. "I never told you I had a brother."

"But you told Jessica, and she mentioned to me that you hadn't seen your brother since your first marriage began. Mr. and Mrs. Lincoln Garland live not far from here, actually. I had my man track them down and sent a carriage to collect them. I thought they could stay with us for a little while before we go back to London and Mr. Garland to his work."

Gillian threw herself into his arms and hugged him tightly. "Thank you. I always wondered what had happened to Lincoln."

Nicolas drew back and grinned. "Mr. Garland is a solicitor. Quite important, I understand. He married a woman from a prominent legal family and has two small boys now."

"I have nephews?"

"*We* have nephews," he corrected her. If she had to cope with his unruly adult children and grandchildren, then it was only fair that he should accept responsibility for hers too. There was much he could do for his wife's brother, not that she would ever ask him for anything to help them. "I'm looking forward to meeting them. I'm keen to hear what Garland has to say about your childhood. I can't believe you were always as perfect as you are now."

"Oh, no. He's going to spoil the illusion I've so deviously woven," Gillian bemoaned, but laughed heartily. "You are the most wonderful husband, Nicolas."

The most wonderful thing about his marriage to Gillian was that being serious had become entirely optional. Now there was no reason to behave, they teased each other a lot.

"I know," Nicolas whispered before giving her a lingering kiss, a prelude to how they might spend the next few uninterrupted hours.

He tugged Gillian into the duchess' bedchamber, and pulled her into his arms.

"What are you up to, your grace?" she asked with one brow arched.

Servants streamed in and out of her new bedchamber, a room that connected to his, but he didn't care who saw them now. There was no scandal since they were well and truly matched and married.

He grinned and caught her hand so he could toy with the wedding band on her finger. "One of the perks of being a married man is that I get to follow you everywhere, your grace."

She twined her fingers with his and leaned into him as the last servant departed. "My favorite is that I may kiss you without waiting for mistletoe anymore."

So she did, and very thoroughly too.

———◆———

If you enjoyed The Duke and I don't miss the
next Saints and Sinners romance

A Gentleman's Vow

ISBN: 978-1-925239-47-8

More Regency Romance from
Heather Boyd...

———•———

And many more

About Heather Boyd

———•———

Determined to escape the Aussie sun on a scorching camping holiday, Heather picked up a pen and notebook from a corner store and started writing her very first novel—Chills. Years later, she is the author of over thirty romances and publisher of several anthologies too. Addicted to all things tech (never again will Heather write a novel longhand) and fascinated by English society of the early 1800's, Heather spends her days getting her characters in and out of trouble and into bed together (if they make it that far). She lives on the edge of beautiful Lake Macquarie, Australia with her trio of mischievous rogues (husband and two sons) along with one rescued cat whose only interest in her career is that it provides him with food on demand.

You can find details of her writing at
www.Heather-Boyd.com